When the elevato

myself short not to step on her. There was Bunny Frank—the buying office big shot—lying diagonally across the car. Her legs were splayed out, and her back was propped against the corner. Her sightless eyes were wide open, and her arms reached out in a come to me baby pose. She was trussed up with shipping tape like a dressed Thanksgiving turkey ready for the oven with a bikini stuffed in her mouth. A Gotham Swimwear hangtag drooped off her lower lip like a toe tag gone lost. Naturally, I burst out laughing.

Before you label me incredibly weird or stone-cold, let me say genetics aren't all they're cracked up to be. If you're lucky, you inherit your Aunt Bertha's sexy long legs or your father's ability to add a bazillion dollar order in his head and get the total correct to the last penny. Without even breaking into a sweat, it's easy to spout at least a million fabulous traits inheritable by the luck of the draw. Did I get those sexy long legs or the ability to add more than two plus two without a calculator? Nooooooooooo. Lucky me. I inherited my Nana's fear of death we overcompensated for with the nervous habit of laughing. A hysterical reaction? Think Bozo the clown eulogizing your favorite aunt.

I craned my neck like a tortoise and checked around. Then I clamped a fist over my mouth. Cripes, how could I possibly explain my guffaws with Bunny lying there? Disappointment was simultaneously mixed with relief when there was no one else in the parking lot. Where was security when you needed them?

Praise for Death by Sample Size:

"Fashion and foul play converge in this fabulous new cozy mystery series." *~Melissa Bourbon, best- selling author the Magical Dressmaking Mysteries,*

~*~

"Death by Sample Size relates the perilous adventures of ladies' swimwear sales executive Holly Shlivnik. When nasty buyer Bunny Frank is found dead and Holly's colleagues are implicated, she sets on the trail of a ruthless killer. Details about the wholesale fashion industry are a bonus while you're trying to figure out whodunit. The well-drawn suspects kept me guessing, and I especially enjoyed the heroine's unique outlook on life. Holly is a hoot! This is one humorous cozy mystery you won't want to miss." *~Nancy J. Cohen, the Bad Hair Day Mysteries*

~*~

"Susie Black makes an entertaining splash with her debut novel. With lively, quirky characters and a wise-cracking sleuth, the story crackles with energy." *~Charlotte Rains Dixon, Emma Jean's Bad Behavior*

~*~

"This is a funny and thoroughly enjoyable cozy mystery from a debut author. I highly recommend it and am looking forward to the next one!" *~Dianne Harman, USA Today Bestselling Author*

~*~

"A hoot-and-a-half. The Holly Swimsuit Mystery series comes in only one size—XX Fun! With a cast of colorful characters and snappy dialogue, Death by Sample Size had me turning the pages. I did not see that ending coming! I can't wait for the next installment."
~Kim Hunt Harris, Trailer Park Princess mysteries

Death by Sample Size

by

Susie Black

A Holly Swimsuit Mystery, Book 1

This is a work of fiction. Names, characters, places, and incidents are either the product of the author's imagination or are used fictitiously, and any resemblance to actual persons living or dead, business establishments, events, or locales, is entirely coincidental.

Death by Sample Size

Contact Information: info@thewildrosepress.com

Cover Art by *Debbie Taylor*

The Wild Rose Press, Inc.
PO Box 708
Adams Basin, NY 14410-0708
Visit us at www.thewildrosepress.com

Publishing History
First Edition, 2021
Trade Paperback ISBN 978-1-5092-3635-0
Digital ISBN 978-1-5092-3636-7

A Holly Swimsuit Mystery, Book 1
Published in the United States of America

Dedication

This book is dedicated to my mentor and dad who saw in me what I didn't see in myself and encouraged me to always reach beyond my grasp. I have stories to tell because he taught me to keep my head on a swivel, and my eyes and heart open to possibilities.

Chapter One

Before the first inkling of dawn, I said good morning to the nosy crane I shared my slip with as I hoisted myself over my houseboat's forward deck. The halyards tinkled a soft sonata on my neighbors' masts as the leeward wind luffed their sails. Damp fingers of morning fog curled over the dock and gave the briny air a chewy texture as I made my way to the gangplank.

I entered the parking structure and dropped the top on my sixty-five pink mustang convertible. I settled into the worn bucket seat and cranked the heater to the blast furnace level. I hit the radio button for the oldies station and jammed the volume loud enough to wake the dead. I crossed Admiralty Way and glugged a fortifying gulp of unleaded commuter mug coffee strong enough to peel two coats of paint off my car.

It's not like I'm even a morning person. But if you're from LA, the one thing you can always count on is you're gonna be stuck in traffic on the 405 whether you're driving at three in the morning or three in the afternoon. The reality is either you're gonna be two hours late or two days early. Such is the life for us LALA Land commuters. What are ya gonna do? I traversed the Marina Freeway and merged into the heavy traffic already bottlenecked on the northbound 405. I crept along at a turtle's pace for three miles until I transitioned eastbound onto I-10 and crawled my way downtown.

****

I finally arrived at the California Apparel Mart minutes before being on the road long enough to become the butt of the old joke I was a young woman when the day began. My footfalls echoed in the near-empty underground parking garage.

I got to the elevator bank and pressed the button. When the elevator doors opened, I had to stop myself short not to step on her. There was Bunny Frank—the buying office big shot—lying diagonally across the car. Her legs were splayed out, and her back was propped against the corner. Her sightless eyes were wide open, and her arms reached out in a come to me baby pose. She was trussed up with shipping tape like a dressed Thanksgiving turkey ready for the oven with a bikini stuffed in her mouth. A Gotham Swimwear hangtag drooped off her lower lip like a toe tag gone lost. Naturally, I burst out laughing.

Before you label me incredibly weird or stone-cold, let me say genetics aren't all they're cracked up to be. If you're lucky you inherit your Aunt Bertha's sexy long legs or your father's ability to add a bazillion dollar order in his head and get the total correct to the last penny. Without even breaking into a sweat, it's easy to spout at least a million fabulous traits inheritable by the luck of the draw. Did I get those sexy long legs or the ability to add more than two plus two without a calculator? Nooooooooo. Lucky me. I inherited my Nana's fear of death we overcompensated for with the nervous habit of laughing. A hysterical reaction? Think Bozo the clown eulogizing your favorite aunt.

I craned my neck like a tortoise and checked

around. Then I clamped a fist over my mouth. Cripes, how could I possibly explain my guffaws with Bunny lying there? Disappointment was simultaneously mixed with relief when there was no one else in the parking lot. Where was security when you needed them?

I toed the elevator door open and bent over Bunny. I'd seen enough CSI episodes to know not to touch her. She was stiff as a board, and I attributed the bluish tinge of her skin to the bikini crammed down her throat. I was no doctor, but I didn't need an MD after my name to make this diagnosis. Bunny Frank was dead as the proverbial doornail.

This was my first time almost tripping over a corpse, so, if there was one, the protocol wasn't clear. Send Bunny to the lobby? As if. Since the lobby wasn't an option, I pressed the stop button. Of course, every ten seconds the darned elevator pinged loudly as though begging me to let it complete its journey.

I was pretty freaked out, babbling to the body. "I should go for help, but I don't wanna leave you here alone." Naturally, Bunny Frank remained mute. She was way beyond giving a crap what I did or didn't do.

I leaned over and read the name on the hangtag out loud in case she was interested in which brand bikini she had lodged in her mouth. "Gotham Swimwear; a sample size ten. I'm gonna take a wild guess the style didn't make it to your retailers' gotta get it on your floor list?" For someone never at a loss for words, Bunny Frank was mum as a cloistered nun. "With you, the problem is the style was probably a real dog and it still made the must-buy list."

After the elevator made its millionth ping, Ernesto, the hunched over, ancient security guard shuffled his way to the elevator bank. His wrinkled skin, the color of cracked clay, was partially hidden under a faded maroon uniform hung two sizes too big on his bony frame.

The big surprise was he even responded. He was normally holed up in the guard shack glued to the novellas on Estrella TV. Why let anything as mundane as an out of order elevator interrupt a juicy program? When you needed him to do something, he either became deaf as a post or lost his ability to understand English. It didn't matter. The old guy was incapable of stopping a wayward bicycle let alone a real intruder. If you were actually in trouble, he'd be the last one to call.

Ernesto stopped at the elevator. He wore an extremely annoyed expression creasing his already wrinkled face. He snapped, "Dis door pingin' ten minutes. Mees Holly, whatssamatta wid you?" He pointed a gnarled index finger across the parking structure and pinned me with an accusatory glare. "You pipple suppose use freight elevator for da samples."

His false teeth shifted, making it even harder to understand him as he clucked his disapproving tongue. "You loading racks? How many you load? Dis long a wait ya got more den two racks. You gonna break da ting ya overload it. Send dis one den make da second trip. Already one elevator es broke. Lotta pipple gonna be mad waiting and yell on me. I no need no troubles wid da *jefe*. Send da ting now. Dis one godda be in da lobby right away."

I stepped in front of Ernesto when he leaned in to release the stop button. "Call the cops. The only thing loaded in there is a dead body."

Ernesto blinked at me in confusion. As comprehension mixed with doubt set in, he peered over my shoulder and gagged. Moving faster than I ever imagined him capable, Ernesto yanked the walkie talkie off his work belt and shouted something resembling Spanglish into the mouthpiece. Sounding like a Chihuahua on steroids, he barked out a call for help.

My eyes had a mind of their own as they strayed over to Bunny. I'd swear she was staring disdainfully back at me as though somehow I'd let her down. As if. Inside my head, Bunny snickered, "Oh, get over yourself."

Before I go any further with this tale, I should introduce myself and explain how I fit into the story. I am Holly Schlivnik, Vice President of Sales at Ditzy Swimwear. I'd recently moved back to LA from Atlanta when I first met Bunny. My apparel career began as a sub rep working for my father traveling the southern states. Rob Bachmann was the owner of Ditzy Swimwear, one of the lines dad and I represented. Rob promoted me to Vice President of Sales and brought me west to the executive office.

In a weird twist of fate and proof positive things never turn out the way you think they will, my dad was now actually working for me. Don't ask; believe me, he got the better end of the deal. The Great God of Guilt fed my mother, so, what do you think? Talk about job security. You should all be so lucky. And they say God doesn't have a sense of humor. Ha. I am living proof God has a rather perverted one.

It was no surprise Bunny Frank had finally pushed someone beyond their limits. The only surprise was it had taken so long. The question wasn't who wanted Bunny Frank dead. The question was who didn't?

Chapter Two

I should have known she'd be trouble by the way she imperiously swept in like she owned the place. Bunny Frank strutted three-quarters of the way into the Ditzy Swimwear showroom and stopped in her tracks. She counted the staff as though she were taking attendance. Who was she expecting? Calvin Klein? As if she was a mind reader, Bunny waved dismissively. Without so much as a hello, she spoke in the same demanding manner like she was addressing the chambermaid. "And where may I ask is my Rob?"

My Rob?

Showroom manager Hope Greenberg gave Bunny a hundred-thousand-watt smile. "Bunny, Rob isn't here." Hope tapped my shoulder. "I'd like to introduce you to our Vice President of Sales, Holly Schlivnik. Holly will be working with you going forward."

During the first week of the new swimwear season, Hope, Buster Schumansky, our LA sales rep, and I had been meeting with local buying office buyers in our showroom at the California Apparel Mart. The mart is a three-building complex of wholesale showrooms occupying an entire city block in downtown Los Angeles.

Buying offices are the eyes and ears of apparel retailers and are located in the major fashion hubs of Dallas, Los Angeles, and New York. For a fee, they provide retailers with a variety of services such as reporting the hottest new trends, as well as negotiating special programs with vendors for their accounts.

Bunny examined me as though she was appraising a side of beef. “This is simply not acceptable.” Bunny’s haughty glare at our showroom manager could have bent steel. “Hope, you know I only work with company principals.” Bunny took a gorgeous leather-bound day planner out of her designer briefcase and pointed the calendar at the phone on the reception desk. She commanded, “Get Rob on the phone this instant. We need to reschedule.”

Bunny flipped her wrist as though with a wave I’d be out of her hair. She sniffed. “I’m sorry, Dolly, but I don’t work with powerless underlings with no authority to make a deal.” Bunny tapped the face of a diamond-studded watch. “Time is money. I can’t wait around while you run to Rob to authorize my agreements. It’s simply more efficient for me to work directly with principals from the start.” She faux apologized, “I’m sorry, but you do understand?”

Powerless underling my Aunt Fanny’s tush. Who the Sam Hill did she think she was talking to? I’d come a long way from being intimidated by pushy buyers who thought only theirs didn’t stink. I can spar with the best and hold my own with a self-absorbed one like her.

Two can play the let’s disrespect the enemy for the control game. I flashed Bunny a killer smile. “For the record, Honey, my name is Holly, not Dolly. Nothing is more constant than change, and things have changed here at Ditzy.” I pointed to the rack of samples hanging behind a work station. “Our business is booming, and Rob is too busy in production to work with accounts. This is why he hired me. Rob has given me the complete authority to negotiate all agreements. I don't need to consult with him on anything before I make a deal. You're right, though." I took the first group of samples off the rack. "Time is money, so why don't we get going?"

I bit my tongue to stop gloating. Bunny's wordless lips moved like a parched guppy. But my victory was short-lived. It didn't take Bunny long to regain her composure. "Although I do speak perfect English, obviously, I didn't make myself clear. So, let me spell it out for you. I don't work with lackeys, no matter how fancy a title is on their business card." Bunny pointed to the phone again. "Get Rob on the line. We have to straighten this out." Her tone was nasty as she taunted me with my own words. "Or since your business is booming, maybe Ditzy Swimwear doesn't need any orders from my accounts."

I took a few beats before I responded. Until five minutes earlier, I didn't know Bunny Frank from Bugs Bunny. I had to be careful. I wasn't always the best at controlling my tongue. Bunny Frank might be an arrogant jerk, but it served no purpose to cut off my nose to spite my face. I consulted my colleagues for their gauge of the situation. Buster angled his head sideways so Bunny didn't see him choking back a guffaw. Hope's eyes had widened when I first challenged Bunny, but now, she quirked a Mona Lisa smile.

Somebody had to put this professional pain in the patootie in her place. Guess I got the honors. I mentally shoved my hand over Dad's mouth to drown out his whispering inside my head. "Don't get mad. Get even by taking their money." Not this time, Daddy. I've gotta set the rules with this one right now, and I've gotta do it my way. "Since we agree time is money, let me bottom line it for you. If you want to offer your accounts any exclusive programs from Ditzy Swimwear, the only way you'll get them is to work it out with me." I flashed Bunny another killer smile. "Are you ready to work or not?"

Bunny's jaw dropped so far it came precariously close to hitting her girls. Apparently, no one had ever spoken to the great Bunny Frank like that before. Bunny sought out Buster and Hope for help. Someone better explain to this upstart interloper exactly who she was talking to. Bunny's gape morphed into an industrial-strength scowl as Buster and Hope shrugged their inability to help her.

Checkmate. Time for Bunny Frank to put up or shut up. Either leave the showroom or get with the program. Beaming a murderous glare in my direction, a glowering Bunny Frank slammed her briefcase on the workstation table and reluctantly took a seat.

I mentally flipped her off as I shoved the line list in front of her nose.

Chapter Three

The annual International Swimwear and Activewear Market (ISAM) culminated with a gala party and fashion show at Global World Studios. Party revelers received badges designed like movie theater ticket stubs as they entered a sound stage featuring a faux movie set. As ISAM special event committee members, Queenie Levine, Michael Rothman, Ronnie Schwartzman, and I costumed and directed the retailers as they read from a short script while a videographer filmed them. A sign adjacent to the set instructed the wannabe stars and starlets to complete a production order and retrieve their movie clip from the producer as they left the sound stage at the party's end.

Royal Swimwear Vice President Queenie Levine was a dark-haired compact dynamo with eyes the color of green tea. She had an athletic build, a sharp wit, and a sharper tongue. We'd met at an ISAM meeting where we were the only female representatives of any member companies. We quickly bonded and became friends in addition to being colleagues.

Not the brightest star in the sky, Michael Rothman was the boyishly handsome National Sales Manager of Dot Junior Swimwear. Michael's big claim to fame was his incorporation of blowing balloon figures as part of his sales presentations.

Ronnie Schwartzman was the arrogant, powerful Western Regional Sales Manager for the mega label conglomerate Clothing Concepts and without any question, the luckiest guy in the swimwear industry. Clothing Concepts owner Martin Decker rewarded Ronnie for being one of the original four company salesmen with the gift of a five percent equity position in the huge company. Good to be king.

Sue Ellen Magee, the no-nonsense, my time is valuable and yours isn't spitfire of a swimwear buyer at Bainbridge Department Stores, walked into the sound stage and headed for the buffet. With a cocky attitude and a razor-edged tongue to match, nasty Sue Ellen was the person for whom the expression words kill surely must have been coined.

Queenie pointed to Sue Ellen. "Can you believe the stunt Bunny pulled on Sue Ellen?"

I rolled my eyes. "I bet Ms. Magee had some major tap-dancing to do for her boss."

An erroneous rumor had raced through the mart saying Bainbridge was being acquired by Allied American Stores and once the acquisition was completed, all Bainbridge executives would be fired. Bunny made the rounds on the swimwear floor with a fabricated story. Sue Ellen was getting out of Bainbridge while the getting was good and had accepted a huge job at the Frank of California buying office.

Sue Ellen and Bunny working together? The concept made me dizzy. "Sorry, Bunny might have been selling but I wasn't buying."

Queenie patted her cheeks. "No kidding. Imagine those two joining forces?"

I burst out laughing. "As if. It would be like General Patton joining forces with Snidely Whiplash.

Sue Ellen is tough, abrasive, and abrupt, but she is as straight as they come. She would never associate herself with the shenanigans Bunny pulls."

Queenie agreed. "No truer words have been spoken. Sue Ellen and Bunny have a long, storied history. They were in the Bainbridge executive training program together."

I almost dropped the boogieboard prop on my foot. "No way."

Queenie's grin was as wide as a Cheshire cat. "Oh yeah, way. And they were in the same division and worked for the same merchandise manager after graduation. You can imagine how they got along. Like oil and water. The two were so busy bickering, they never got any work done. The infighting was so disruptive, their manager transferred Sue Ellen to a different division." Queenie snickered, "Imagine if Bunny was Sue Ellen's boss? Sue Ellen cowtowing to Bunny?" Queenie howled like a coyote. "Oh yeah; pigs will sooner grow wings. If the rumor had been true, I wouldn't have given the marriage a week."

I squeaked like a mouse. "A week? I wouldn't have given it a full day. By lunchtime, Sue Ellen would have run Bunny through a woodchipper."

Michael laughed. "The Iron Maiden definitely had some chinks in her armor to patch."

Ronnie rubbed his hands together. "It wasn't even the worst part."

I narrowed my eyes. "What do you mean?"

Ronnie wiggled his brows. "Sue Ellen was in line for a management promotion. Till this happened, the promotion was practically a done deal. As of now, it's been indefinitely postponed. When I spoke to Sue

Ellen, she was spitting bullets." Ronnie did a one-eighty around the sound stage and shuddered. "I'd hate to be Bunny when Sue Ellen gets a hold of her."

No kidding. Sue Ellen Magee was not someone you wanted for an enemy.

I panned the group. "You guys have any problems with Bunny? Some of the stories out in the market are way over the top."

Michael smiled sheepishly. "Yeah, she's hustled me some and threatened to keep Dot off her infamous gotta have it on your floor list if we didn't come across with some favors."

I hid my amusement behind a script when Queenie gave me the big eyes. On the first night of the swimwear market, there was no question of the type of favors Bunny expected from Michael. Ca-Ching. Queenie and I were walking to our cars in the mart garage. Michael was parked several rows ahead of us. Bunny got out of the elevator and stopped at Michael's car. We overheard Bunny tell Michael if he wanted Dot to get any business from her accounts, he better have a lot of dead Presidents for her. Michael replied Dot was a hot line and he didn't need to pay her off to get business from her stores. Bunny laughed hysterically; the last time Dot had a hot number, Annette Funicello was doing the horizontal hula with Frankie Avalon. Michael still didn't fork over the greenbacks, so Bunny wished him good luck and walked off. Bunny got twenty feet away when Michael called her back and slapped a fat envelope into her hand.

Queenie took a script back from an actor and pointed it at Ronnie. "And what's your story?"

Ronnie had become too intent on reorganizing the costumes in their proper order on a rolling rack to respond. In case he missed her question, Queenie smacked Ronnie on the shoulder with the script. "A big company like yours must pay through the nose to get all those major commitments locked in."

Ronnie smiled tightly. "Clothing Concepts doesn't have to resort to payoffs to get its business."

When the last of the future Oscar nominees had finally completed their film debuts, Michael and Ronnie quickly said their good-byes and practically pole-vaulted to the bar.

I blew out my cheeks. "We definitely hit some sore spots. Both of them were squirming big time."

Queenie crossed her arms over her chest. "Trust me; those two are paying Bunny off bigly. No one gets any business from Bunny Frank without paying the piper. Bunny doesn't care whether or not your line is the latest and greatest. The only thing important to Bunny Frank is what's in it for her."

I blinked my surprise. "Royal pays Bunny off?"

Queenie slapped the costume rack and laughed. "I work for the two biggest connivers in the business. What do you think?" She arched a brow. "And if Ditzy does any business with Bunny, I guarantee she has her hand deeply embedded in your boss' pocket."

No wonder Bunny was so insistent on working with Rob.

Chapter Four

With our ISAM obligations completed, I was ready for some food and fun. I scanned the packed sound stage for any open tables, but there wasn't an empty chair. "Do you see any open places?" I fingered the collar of my silk jacket and shuddered. "Standing and getting bumped trying to eat messy finger food off those dinky paper plates is a disaster waiting to happen."

Queenie pointed to the back of the sound stage. "The yentas are at a table behind the buffet. Maybe they saved us seats."

The yentas, Joan Binder, Hope Greenberg, Queenie Levine, Sonia Wilson, and I had been meeting each morning for coffee for six months. What began as a once in a while get together had morphed into the glue binding our group of colleagues to one another.

At forty-five, Joan Binder was the oldest yenta. Vivacious, quick-witted, hennaed Joan had been the Royal Swimwear showroom manager for twenty years.

Emerald-eyed, ash-blonde Hope Greenberg was on the shady side of her thirties. Hope was a big girl; big-boned, big feet, big busted, and, ironically selling tiny bikinis when she was, to be kind, rather plump. She was one of those girls who had been told too many times to count what a shame; with such a beautiful face…if she'd drop the weight, she'd be a knockout.

After escaping a rotten marriage leaving her to raise two young children alone, dirty blonde, brown-eyed Itsy-Bitsy Bikini National Sales Manager Sonia Wilson quickly learned to survive. Sonia's showroom was next to ours. An occasional sharing of office supplies and industry gossip blossomed into a close friendship.

Queenie and I pushed our way through the mob stuffing their faces at the buffet and got to the yentas' table. Good to have friends like the yentas. They saved us seats and had plates of food and glasses of wine waiting for us.

We slid into our seats, and Joan wrinkled her nose. "Please accept my sympathies; you two were stuck working with Michael and Ronnie for over an hour." She laughed. "Did they talk about anything besides football and beer?"

My grin was devilish. "Oh, yeah. The stunt Bunny pulled on Sue Ellen last week."

Joan's pageboy-styled hairdo curtained her striking violet eyes as she shook her head. "What on God's green Earth was going through Bunny Frank's mind to dream up such a whopper?"

Sonia puckered her lips. "I'm not the least bit surprised by any stunt she pulls." She spat, "Bunny Frank is one manipulative, conniving bitch."

Queenie and I shared a sideways glance.

Queenie pointed a bacon-wrapped prawn at Bunny Frank muscling her way into the front of the buffet line. "Bunny must be starving." Queenie smirked. "It's hard work stealing your competition's clients right out from under their noses."

Hope blew out her cheeks. "What did she do now?"

I said, "Bunny stationed herself at a spot right after you got through the turnstiles. We had to go past her to get to the sound stage. We caught her whole spiel."

Hope furrowed her brow. "Spiel? What schtick could she pull at a party?"

Queenie said, "She had an armful of her company portfolios and was working the crowd as the retailers entered the park."

Joan peered over her glasses. "You're joking. She buttonholed retailers here?"

Queenie rolled her eyes. "Oh yeah. Big time."

I crossed my heart. "No lie. The woman campaigned like she was running for Congress."

Hope sighed. "Good grief."

In one of those cosmically strange cases of it is indeed a small world, after all, Hope Greenberg and Bunny Frank had a relationship spanning more than a decade. Both women had been Phi Sigma Delta Alumna sorority sisters at Wayne State University in Detroit.

No two women were more the opposite of one another. Hope, with her beautiful heart-shaped face and heavyset body, personified those Midwest values of openness and honesty sometimes making her seem like a homer. With her ugly face and sexpot figure, Bunny shed those Midwest values when she crossed the California state line. Despite their differences, reunited post-college via the Los Angeles apparel industry, the two remained friends. Hope served as Bunny's conscience and Bunny Hope's vicarious walk on the wild side with no consequences.

Sonia snapped, "Who was the victim this time?"

I said, "She sidled over to some guy named Barnes. She yammered on and on and wouldn't let him go until he took one of her company portfolios."

Joan's jaw dropped. "Older guy, patrician nose, snooty talker?"

I nodded. "Yeah, he's the guy."

Joan's eyes widened as big as silver dollars. "You must be kidding. He's the one she was buttonholing?"

I asked, "I take it you know him?"

Joan snorted. "Doesn't everyone? She hustled Jethro Barnes, the CEO of Diamond's Department Stores."

I said, "When Barnes was finally able to pry himself away from her, he went right over to Osborne Bradley and Ellen Thomas from Acme and showed them Bunny's portfolio."

Joan said, "I'm not surprised. Diamond's is one of Acme Buying office's biggest accounts."

Queenie twirled a straw between her fingers. "It certainly explains a lot. Ellen's reaction was pretty intense. She grabbed the portfolio out of the guy's hand and stormed over to Bunny and got in her face."

I said, "Ellen's waving the portfolio like a crazy woman and threatening Bunny big time."

Hope's eyes bugged. "Dear lord, what did Bunny do?"

Sonia muttered, "I wouldn't put it past Bunny to haul off and slug her."

I shook my head. "Nope. Bunny threw her head back and laughed."

Sonia sucked in her cheeks as if she'd bitten into a sour pickle. "It's a wonder someone hasn't given Bunny Frank exactly what she deserves."

Chapter Five

I cleaned every morsel off my plate and helped myself to half of Queenie's, and my stomach was still growling. I went to scrounge through any leftovers at the buffet, but the line still snaked back to the sound stage entrance. Would there be anything left by the time I got to the buffet? Doubtful. Was Bunny still in line? Maybe she'd take pity on me and let me cut in. I scoured the crowd, but Bunny wasn't in it. I got behind Clothing Concepts' head designer Louis Chennault and Carefree Casuals swimwear buyer Angela Wellborn at the end of the line and hoped for the best.

Despite his imperfections, or perhaps because of them, women were drawn to fiftyish Louis Chennault like moths to a flame. He had a widow's peak of receding curly black hair with a touch of gray at the temples. He sported a salt and pepper Van Dyke beard and had crooked front teeth behind full, kissable lips. His piercing, hooded dark eyes guarded a bent nose. He wore a tiny amplifier embedded in his right ear and spoke with a charming British accent. His rep was he had an eye for younger women and a European-bred superior attitude of teaching those American sloths how to dress. Chennault rested his hand in the small of Angela's back and leaned over to say something to her. Thirtyish Angela, with her boxy, mannish physique and dull, forgettable features, hung on Louis like a shroud.

When the fashion show was over, the music started, and partiers flocked to the dance floor. Angela and Louis were dancing cheek to cheek. Queenie wrinkled her nose. "Louis and Angela have been inseparable tonight. Are those two like an item?"

Was she out of her mind? I sputtered, "Oh, come on, get real. Angela's one of the nicest people in the industry, but she's not exactly the type he goes for. The word is Louis Chennault likes them hot and stacked." Bunny stood at the bar and stared at Louis and Angela dancing. "Bunny's more Louis' speed, but you can never tell. They say opposites attract."

Joan agreed. "They must. Louis and Angela are together when I arrive at A Jolt of Java every morning."

I choked on my wine. "No way."

Joan entwined her baby fingers and pulled on them in a pinkie swear. "Yeah, way. I'm telling you; they are together all the time."

Sonia added her two cents. "And Angela goes into the Gotham showroom whenever she's on our aisle."

Hope reasoned, "Gotham must be her biggest supplier. It's no surprise she spends a lot of time there."

Sonia simpered, "Trust me; she's doing more than placing orders."

Queenie gave Angela the once-over. "She's certainly different from the Angela we're used to. She's sporting a zippy new hairdo, wearing make-up, and her boobs are a lot bigger, so unless she had plastic surgery, she must be wearing a padded bra, and hallelujah; she ditched those frumpy, old lady floral print dresses even my grandmother wouldn't wear."

Joan drummed a spoon on the table. "It must be the Professor Higgins effect they say Louis has on the ladies. He's got a rep to doll the duller ones up."

Queenie reminded me of my Nana when she tapped the tip of her nose with her index finger. "They're involved in something all right. Angela and Louis were seated two tables away from mine last Wednesday at the mart deli. They split the sky-high pastrami on rye and a big share of giggles on the side."

Joan chortled, "Oh yeah, she's got it bad. She has the Nancy Reagan adoration look written all over her face."

I mused out loud. "She's such a nice woman. I hope he doesn't hurt her."

Hope pursed her lips. "When Angela's not facing him, he isn't as smitten with her."

Hope was right. Louis was checking out the other women on the dance floor. As Clothing Concepts CEO Martin Decker and his trophy wife Shannon glided past Louis and Angela, I caught the glance Louis and Mrs. Decker shared. "Louis is definitely into something."

Queenie surveyed the group. "The question is what?"

The DJ announced the first buses back to the mart were leaving in fifteen minutes. A third of the crowd made its way out of the sound stage. Louis draped his arm across Angela's shoulder as he walked her to the exit. He gave her a chaste kiss on the cheek and went back to the party.

Bunny Frank hadn't moved an inch from her spot at the bar. As the music resumed, Bunny knocked back her last shot and checked out the room. She zig-zagged across the soundstage to where Louis Chennault stood two tables away from ours. He held a drink and had an arm wrapped around the waist of a buxom bleach-bottle-blonde poured into a skin-tight mini skirt and a flimsy tank top.

Bunny inserted herself between Louis and the blonde. "Take a hike, honey. This one's spoken for. Go find someone else to play with."

The blonde gave Bunny a deer in the headlights, and Bunny elbowed the confused young woman out of the way. The blonde peeled Louis' fingers off her waist and stomped to the bar. Bewildered, Louis called after her, "Brigette, baby cakes, what did I do? Come back." The blonde gave Louis the middle finger salute.

Bunny hooked her arms around Louis' neck and slurred a loudish coo. "Hellooo, baby. I've missed you something awful Louie, Louie."

Louis unwrapped Bunny's arms from his neck and pointed to the blonde. "What did you say to her?"

Bunny made a Betty Boop moue with her wormy lips. "I told her to take a hike. You're taken and she should find someone else to play with."

Bunny tugged Louis toward the dance floor. "Come on, dance with me, and let's see what else we come up with to do. It's been way too long."

Louis growled, "You and I have been over for ages. Caput, done, finished." Exasperation shrilled the tone of his voice. "How many ways must I say you are yesterday's news?"

Louis pushed Bunny aside and stalked to the bar. Sloppy from all the booze, Bunny stumbled as she chased after him, but she caught Louis by the arm and spun him around. Before Louis realized what was happening, Bunny grabbed the drink out of his hand

and threw it in his face. The party dins died as guests stopped to take in the action.

Bunny waved the empty glass at Louis and screamed, "No one says no to Bunny Frank. No one." She bared her teeth like a rabid dog. "I promise, you will live to regret it."

Queenie cackled, "Forget the movie stars on the backlot. Bunny Frank was the entertainment for this party."

Chapter Six

Margaret Adams, Bunny Frank's Plain-Jane office manager, left the barista's counter and stopped at our table. Margaret set a greasy paper bag and a couple of to-go cups of coffee on the table and sat next to Joan. She bussed Joan's cheek and flashed the rest of the group a toothy grin.

Joan air-kissed Margaret. "Mags, long time no see."

Margaret pulled a fuzzy cardigan around her narrow shoulders and barked a throaty laugh. "I don't get out much. The wicked witch of east ninth street normally keeps me chained to my desk."

Queenie joked, "So, you're out on good behavior?"

Margaret shook her head. "Nah, I'm on a mission of mercy. Her Royal Highness was at Cedars Sinai hospital all night with her sister. Poor Sandra had an epileptic seizure off the charts. Bunny came straight to the office from the hospital. The last time she ate was lunch yesterday." Margaret pointed to the grease-stained bag with the mart deli logo. "The Queen of mean is a lot crankier than usual when she doesn't get her three squares. Her Royal Highness didn't like the delivery time the deli quoted, so she sent me out to fetch her breakfast." Margaret smiled elfishly. "She must be exhausted. Her Majesty ordered breakfast for me too."

I choked on my coffee. "Bunny has a sister?" My eyes widened. "You mean she wasn't the devil's spawn?"

Hope explained, "Sandra is Bunny's older sister. When their parents followed Bunny west from Michigan, Sandra came too. The parents are long gone, and there's nobody else."

"Yes, it's only the two of them." Margaret sighed. "It's a sad story. Sandra has advanced MS and can't take care of herself. She lives with Bunny but needs help in the house when Bunny isn't home." Margaret smiled impishly. "You'd never imagine a self-centered jerk like Bunny Frank gives two hoots for anyone but herself, but she is quite devoted to her sister." Margaret's eyes shone. "Bunny has never forgotten the Cedars Sinai Neurology staff has saved Sandra's life several times. Not only is Bunny one of the hospital's most generous donors, but she is also a tireless fundraiser for the Fashion Industry Guild of Cedars Sinai." Margaret's elfin grin was wicked. "Bunny keeps her generosity and charitable work on the down low. After all, the Queen of mean has a reputation to maintain."

"Another mystery solved." Joan tapped her index finger to the side of her head. "I could never figure out the connection between Bunny and Cedars. The Guild has a huge fundraiser event twice a year, and Bunny hits all the vendors for a major donation." Joan laughed. "Bunny Frank may be a lot of things, but shy she isn't. If she doesn't like the size of your donation, she has no problem telling you to stick your hand back in your pocket and dig a little deeper."

Margaret grabbed the bag and two coffees. "I better hustle my bustle or there will be hell to pay if, God forbid, Her Majesty's egg sandwich is served cold."

As Margaret headed for the exit, she waved a greeting to Angela Wellborn and Louis Chennault, who had taken the table across from ours.

Joan batted her eyes at the couple. "None of us could see those two together, but I guess we don't see too good. The other day Angela came into our showroom to drop off some orders. While we were going over the styles, she gushed over Louis. Turns out Angela and Louis have been involved for a while. They met at a Gotham fashion show after-party last season and discovered they had a common interest in cars. Louis is an amateur race car driver. Angela mentioned her dad's hobby was restoring old cars. Angela laughed she was the son her father never had. The two of them tinkered weekends with her dad's cars when she was a kid."

I slapped the table, and a few drops of coffee sloshed out of my cup. "Which reminds me of something odd. It happened a couple of months ago, and I'd forgotten all about it. One night after work, I got to my car and found Angela Wellborn walking around it. I asked if anything was wrong. She explained no, her dad had a vintage mustang hardtop the same year as my convertible and she was admiring my car." I dabbed the spilled coffee with a sodden napkin and smiled. "She asked what size the engine was, and I had no idea. She wanted to peek under the hood. The request was a strange one, but what the heck, why not? She popped the latch and was under there for twenty minutes having a grand old time checking the valves and pistons and squeezing the hoses."

Joan said, "Angela certainly must have a thing for cars. She and Louis worked several weekends on a pit crew at Laguna Seca Raceway."

Queenie laughed. "Gosh, how much more romantic than a two-minute oil change can a date get?"

Joan shrugged. "To each his own. Angela wiggled her ring finger and whispered don't be surprised if wedding bells are in her future."

As they say in the old south, shut mah mouth.

Chapter Seven

Sonia Wilson's thirty-fourth birthday fell on Friday. The yentas treated the birthday girl to lunch at The Showroom, a trendy yet cozy restaurant located on the second floor of the California Apparel Mart. The Showroom featured the most delicious seafood salad in the city, a fantastic mirrored bar occupying the entire south side of the restaurant, and the best seat in the house to check out all the important apparel industry movers and shakers move and shake.

I'd just closed my menu when Bunny Frank sashayed into the dining room wearing a sexy little black dress cut down to there and back again. Diamond teardrop earrings, a single strand of black pearls, and matching four-inch stilettos practically screaming baby, take me this instant completed her ensemble.

The maître d' led her to a back booth one over from ours. She took a little red velvet box out of her purse with XXIV Carats Jewelers stenciled on the top and put it on the table between the two place settings. She picked the fuller buds of a beautiful bouquet of crimson roses out of a crystal vase in the center of the table and randomly scattered the petals over the embroidered tablecloth. The maître d' set a gorgeous silver candelabra with lit candles next to the flower vase. An expensive bottle of champagne chilled in an ice bucket next to the booth.

I motioned to the elaborate table setting. "Some lucky stiff is getting the Rolls Royce treatment."

Queenie joked, "Whose huge account is she stealing now?"

Mr. Barnes' face flitted across my memory. The guy had shown zero interest in changing buying offices, but with Bunny's infamous powers of persuasion, was it a big stretch to imagine Jethro Barnes as her guest?

A tuxedo-clad violinist rehearsed adjacent to Bunny's booth. I joked, "Is she gonna seduce him or sign him?"

Joan pursed her lips like a funnel. "Definitely seduction. It's how she gets all her male clients to sign on the dotted line."

Sonia sniggered. "No doubt, it's how she keeps 'em." Sonia wiggled her brows. "Ask old Ernie at Carefree Casuals."

Gack. Ernie Naumann opened the first Carefree Casuals store the same year my Uncle Barry went to kindergarten. Ernie was seventy-five if he was a day.

Bunny checked her face in the mirror of her compact, dabbed a spot of powder on her nose, freshened her lipstick, and spritzed herself with a squirt of perfume. As Bunny finished primping, Louis Chennault walked into the restaurant and circulated the room. Angela Wellborn was seated at a table across from us with two other Carefree Casual buyers. Angela gave Louis a million-dollar smile, but he walked right past her with nary a glance. Angela's eyes followed Louis as he made his way across the crowded restaurant. Her eyes popped when Louis stopped at Bunny's table. He took a seat next to Bunny and gave her a polite peck on the cheek.

Hope gasped, “Son of a gun. She actually did it.”

Joan gave Hope a strange look. “Who did what?”

Hope angled her head toward the table next to ours. “Bunny. I had lunch with her after the ISAM party debacle and gave her a piece of my mind. I told her, Bunny, I’ve gotta say, you outdid yourself this time. You made a complete fool of yourself at the party. You were an embarrassment to yourself, your office, your accounts, and the industry.” Hope clucked her tongue in disapproval. “And the little stunt she pulled on Louis Chennault? Good grief. I told her if you don’t want to apologize to your accounts, at least you owe Louis one heck of an apology. She swore she would call Louis and invite him to lunch.” Hope dipped her head to Bunny’s table. “Guess she did.”

Bunny took the bottle out of the ice bucket and poured two flutes of champagne. She handed Louis a flute, lifted hers, and toasted, “To possibilities.” Bunny signaled the violinist, and Louis stared bewildered when the musician strolled to their table playing Sway Me Now.

Louis took stock of the violinist, the flowers, the champagne, and the candles and deadpanned, “You may have gone a teensy bit overboard, but boy, can you apologize.”

Bunny answered with a seductive smile and snuggled closer to Louis. He tried scooting tactfully away, but Bunny had him cornered. Louis shuddered as Bunny caressed the back of his neck.

Bunny put her champagne flute on the table and opened the velvet box, revealing an exquisite diamond and blue star sapphire-encrusted ring. Bunny took the ring out of the box and before Louis realized what she was going to do, she slipped it on his ring finger.

Bunny stroked Louis' hand and gazed into his eyes. "Louis, life is short. Before you turn around, time has passed you by, and you've let the important things get away. I loved you from the moment I laid eyes on you. I loved you when we were together, and I still loved you after we broke up. I never stopped loving you. I love you now more than ever." Bunny patted her girls. "Booze did my talking at the party, and I'm sorry for the way it came out, but I can't apologize for what I feel." Bunny's voice caught. "I am a woman who knows exactly what she wants, and I'm not afraid to reach out and take it." Bunny lifted her champagne flute and pointed it at Louis. "And I want you." Bunny's eyes filled. "Louis, please marry me. I love you, and I want to grow old with you. No two people were more meant to be together, more right for one another. I promise to do my best to make you happy eight days a week."

The slack-jawed yentas were rendered speechless. Who knew Bunny Frank could speak from the heart? Who knew Bunny Frank had a heart? We waited with bated breath for Louis Chennault's answer.

For a moment Louis stared at Bunny dumbstruck. His expression soon changed from utter bewilderment to great amusement. To Bunny's horror, Louis laughed himself silly. His loud, horsey guffaws mocked her as they reverberated like echoes around the packed room. The yentas shrank in their seats, not wanting to add to her embarrassment, but unless Bunny crawled beneath the table, there was no place for her to hide.

Louis sputtered to a stop and wiped his eyes with his napkin. He waved at the violinist to get his attention. Louis drew his index finger across his throat. "Okay, pal." Louis pointed to the violin. "You can put your fiddle back in its case." Louis took a hundred-dollar bill out of his wallet and handed it to the hapless musician, who had continued playing. "Go buy yourself a good meal." The violinist snatched the C-note out of Louis' hand, packed his fiddle, and left quickly before Louis changed his mind. Louis giggled. "Oh, Bunny, your speech was priceless. What a gag. This is fantastic." Louis took the ring off and handed it back to Bunny. He tittered, "Wherever did you get this ring? Can you still get a prize in a box of Cracker Jack?" Louis pointed to the stones set into the ring. "You had me fooled. It's a heck of a fake." He fingered the XXIV Carats jewelry box. "The fancy box is such a good touch." Louis beamed a movie star smile of approval. "Bunny, this is the greatest apology I've ever had. I accept." Louis opened his menu and scanned the selections. "I'm starved. So, what are you gonna eat? The seafood salad here is divine, and those mini garlic croissants it comes with are to die for…"

Tears dribbled her cheeks as Bunny closed her fingers over the ring and choked back a sob. "I can assure you the ring is the real thing." She rotated the ring around for him. "I even paid extra to have it engraved."

In a nanosecond, Louis' demeanor changed from amusement to alarm. "You're serious?"

She snapped, "As a heart attack. I want you, and you're gonna be mine." Bunny wiped the tears off her cheeks and waved the ring in the air like a live grenade. "And trust me, I always get what I want."

Louis closed the menu and threw his napkin on the table. "You're out of your mind. We dated for three months two years ago, for crying out loud. We had some good times, a few romps in the hay, and we were done. Where did you ever get the idea you and I had any future together? It certainly wasn't from me. There never was an us, there is no us, and there never will be an us. Nothing is ever gonna change, no matter how many bouquets or cards you shower me with." Louis scooted to the edge of the booth. "You can't stalk someone into love with you. Like I told you at the party, you are yesterday's news." Louis faced the exit. "Take a reality pill and get outta dreamland. The entertainment was fabulous, but I'm outta here."

Bunny grabbed his arm as he walked away. She spat out the words like a mouthful of watermelon seeds. "Not so fast. You don't realize how perfect I am for you? No matter. You don't love me? Too bad. Get used to it, Louis. You're gonna be mine. I'm gonna have you, one way or the other."

Louis' face contorted with a mixture of pity and contempt. "You're a joke, Bunny, a pathetic old joke. You need to get a life, but you won't be sharing it with me. You were good for some giggles but nothing more. When I was done with you, I tossed you away." Louis pulled Bunny's fingers off his arm and strode out of the restaurant. Angela excused herself, dropped a twenty on the table, and scurried to follow Louis.

Bunny tried on the ring while sipping the rest of her champagne and talked to the bubbly. "Remember at the party Louie, Louie? No one says no to me, no one."

Bunny twirled the ring around her finger. “You will live to regret this, Louie, Louie. Oh yeah, baby, you will.”

Little did we know the pandora’s box Bunny Frank would open.

Sonia Wilson pointed a forkful of birthday cake over at Bunny. “Thank you, yentas. This was the best birthday present I could ever wish for.”

As she’d soon find out, Sonia should have taken my wise Nana’s advice and been more careful what she wished for.

Chapter Eight

Saturday night I met my friend Christine for dinner at Shanghai Star Café, a Chinese-themed restaurant located at the far end of Fisherman's Village. Even with a reservation, we still had a thirty-minute wait. There was nowhere to sit in the crowded reception area. If we didn't want to wait outside in the cold wind, the bar was the last option. Two rows of bright red Chinese lanterns strung across the top of the bar blinked a greeting as we grabbed the last table.

We'd ordered a round of drinks, and Ronnie Schwartzman came into the bar with a stunning blonde hanging on his arm. Ronnie scanned the room and recognized me sitting in the back. I ignored him as he waved to get my attention.

Chris asked, "See the guy at the bar entrance waving at you? Is he a friend of yours?" My pal wasn't one for mincing words. "You can't miss him. He's the dork with the captain's hat who's dressed like the Schweppes Commander Whitehead." She pointed to Ronnie. "See him? He's the big ape with the blonde bimbo draped like a mink stole on his arm."

I choked back a laugh. "Not a friend, but I do know him. Big shot at a major competitor of ours. My showroom's across from his."

Ronnie and the blonde stood next to our table. Nana's voice lectured in my head. "Play nice in the sandbox." I ignored her and plastered a fake smile on my kisser. "Hey, Ronnie, pretty far from Beverly Hills, aren't you? Here slumming?"

Ronnie turned to the blonde and smirked. "Rhoda, meet my smart-alec neighbor from the mart, Holly Schlivnik." Ronnie beamed one of those I don't know who you are but you might be someone important, so I better be nice to you smiles at Chris. "Have we met? Excuse me, but if we have, I don't remember you." Ronnie tipped the bill of his hat. "I'm Ronnie Schwartzman."

Chris smiled at Ronnie. "Nope, we've never met. I'm not in the rag business." Chris extended her right hand, but Ronnie didn't take it. "I'm Holly's friend Chris. Nice to meet you."

Ronnie made a half-assed wave at the blonde. "This is my wife Rhoda."

Rhoda waggled the fingers of her left hand under our noses. The brilliant-cut diamond set in the platinum engagement ring was the size of a door knocker. She sniffed in a haughty tone meaning she wasn't the least bit, "Charmed, I'm sure."

Ronnie tapped a drumbeat on our table. "Hey, you mind sharing?" He pointed to the stack of chairs next to the bar. "I'll ask the bartender to bring over two chairs when I place our drink order?"

I was going to say yes, I minded when Chris kicked me in the shins. Nana had apparently joined us for drinks. I patted the table and tried not to gag. "Don't be silly; of course, we don't mind. Please join us."

Ronnie grinned, "Fantastic. What are you two drinking? The next round is on me."

A few minutes later, the bartender pushed two chairs to the table and delivered the drinks along with a steaming plate of eggrolls.

Ronnie waved around the bar. "This place is one of our favorite hangs. We eat here whenever we've been out on the boat." I mentally crossed Shanghai Star Café off my restaurant list. Ronnie pointed toward the door. "Bought our boat from Marina Yacht sales on Fiji."

I asked, "Is your boat sail or power?"

Ronnie's chest puffed out like a proud papa. "Seventy-five-foot Hatteras."

Rhoda pointed a manicured index finger at me. "Do you live in the marina?"

I said, "I live on a houseboat in the northwest end of the marina."

Rhoda turned to Chris. "You live here, too?"

Chris shook her head. "No, I live in Sherman Oaks out in the valley."

Rhoda wrinkled her nose like she smelled yesterday's garbage and gave Chris the once-over. "And what is it you do?"

Chris said, "I'm a legal secretary for in-house counsel at Craftberry Studios in Burbank." Chris gives it as good as she gets. "Do you work or just spend his money?"

I almost spat out my drink, but Christine's sarcasm was lost on Ronnie's wife. Rhoda's face lit bright as a Christmas tree. She took a sterling silver cardholder from her designer clutch and handed us each an embossed business card. Rhoda crowed like a rooster. "I'm a Beverly Hills realtor. Glamor Properties. Mega mansion division." Rhoda smiled with all the sincerity of a used car salesman. "Last year I was the number one volume agent." Rhoda eyed Chris like she was another appetizer. "I specialize in entertainers and Iranians." She cooed, "Call me. We can help each other. Any referrals you send me who pan out, I'll give you a finder's fee." Rhoda simpered, "Play your cards right and you can make a lot more money with me than you ever will typing."

Ronnie took the last eggroll and shoved it into his mouth whole. "Where's your houseboat moored?"

"Porto Paloma Marina."

He asked, "What basin number?"

I looked at him oddly. "Seventeen hundred. Why?"

Ronnie's eyes widened. "You're kidding. Isn't it a small world? We're in the same marina two basins from you; fifteen hundred, last slip at the end of the dock."

My jaw went slack. "Your boat is the Bikini Mistress? I was always curious if someone from our industry owned her. She's an impressive vessel."

Ronnie stared at Rhoda. "One of us agrees with you."

I asked, "How long have you moored your boat there?"

Ronnie flashed three fingers. "Three years this past summer."

I mused, "I've been in the same slip for a year this coming December. Isn't it odd we've never bumped into one another?"

Rhoda stuck her snooty nose in the air and sniffed haughtily. "We're busy people. Not a lot of free time to waste sitting around on a boat." She smiled tightly. "What do they say? The two happiest days of a boater's life are the day he buys it and the day he sells it."

I deadpanned, "I take it you're not too keen on boating?"

Rhoda pursed her lips. "Hardly. The kids won't step foot on it. They wanted a sailboat. He bought the QE2." Rhoda shuddered. "The slightest motion makes me queasy." She patted her perfectly coiffed hair. "The wind twists my hairdo into so many knots it takes my stylist two hours to untangle it, and the salt air is poison for my delicate skin." She barked out a laugh. "Otherwise, I absolutely adore it."

Leave it to my pal Chris to state the obvious. "So, why do you go?" Chris jutted her chin at Ronnie. "He's a big boy. Can't he take care of himself?"

Rhoda glared at Ronnie. "Oh yeah, he certainly can. Ronald loves the boat, says it relaxes him as nothing else can. There's a reason he calls it his mistress." Rhoda slit her eyes. "I go along to guarantee The Bikini Mistress is the only mistress he has."

Meow. I filed the juicy tidbit away for future reference.

I broke the awkward silence by changing the subject. "Ronnie, I've been meaning to ask. Who did your flowers for the swimwear market? Was it someone from the florist downstairs in the mart? The arrangements were gorgeous and the talk of the aisle. We have a sales meeting next month, and I'd like to use your florist."

Ronnie's proud smile split his face in two. "Our daughter, Jennifer. She's taking horticulture at Beverly Hills High."

Rhoda said, "We'd taken the kids to Royal Gardens on Vancouver Island last summer, and Jen fell in love with flowers. The term project she chose was to create a small version of the Royal Italian flower garden in our backyard."

Ronnie bragged, "She got the highest grade in the class." He grinned. "Of course, it didn't hurt she got some expert advice from one of her dad's customers who happens to be a master gardener."

"Who?"

"Angela Wellborn." Ronnie eyed me strangely. "Don't tell me you haven't been to Angela's office?" He smiled. "It's famous, a step below a tourist stop." His tone was incredulous. "You've never been there?"

I shook my head no. "We always work in the showroom."

Ronnie said, "Find an excuse to work with her at the store. You won't regret it. Her office is amazing. It's like being in a rainforest. She's even got a waterfall." He laughed. "The problem is, the tinkling of the waterfall makes you have to pee all the time."

"I'll have to get out there. It sounds fantastic." I smiled. "Your daughter did one heck of a job. Would you let her work for us? I'll pay her generously for the plants and her time."

Rhoda and Ronnie glanced at one another. "Why not? I'll ask her if she's interested."

I grinned. "Thank you. If she is interested, it would be great."

I pointed my wine glass at the emblem sewn on the breast pocket of Ronnie's blazer. "You're members of the Del Rey Yacht Club?"

Ronnie caressed the emblem like a lover's cheek. "I'm a Charter member and on the board of directors."

I asked, "I'm curious; why don't you moor your boat at the Yacht Club?"

Ronnie sucked in his cheeks and blew out his impatience. "I'm on a waiting list for an end slip. They're the only ones long enough to accommodate a boat as big as mine." Ronnie smirked. "It shouldn't be too much longer. Harold Green is eighty-five, married a big-busted bimbo last year who is sixty years his junior, and he has a bad ticker. With any luck, the bimbo is wearing him out. Neither the wife nor his kids want the boat. When Harold kicks the bucket, his Bertram Flybridge will be history before his body is cold." Ronnie licked his chops. "I'm next on the list for his slip. If things go my way, The Bikini Mistress will be in a new home after the first of the year."

Chapter Nine

Angela Wellborn stood outside our showroom. Normally, she was one of the most even-keeled buyers. But storm clouds were evident as Angela had her hand on the door handle but made no move to open it. Since Angela's feet appeared cemented to the floor, I opened the showroom door for her. Angela's eyes flashed a flicker of pain when I joked, "We don't charge extra if you come in." Curious.

She sat at a workstation and opened a computer report to the page with our styles on it. Angela winced as she asked me to put four styles on the grid. I did as I was told and waited for her explanation. She got right to it. "I'm canceling all the on-order units for those four styles. Business is tough, and my management has told me to get out of these styles."

I did a doubletake. What the Sam Hill was this crap? Those four are our best-selling styles on her floor. Before my brain could stop my mouth from inserting my foot in it, I blurted, "Do you actually read your sales reports?"

Angela flinched as though she'd been slapped. "Yeah, I do. It's how my buying decisions are made." Angela was no dummy, far from it, but even the most dimwitted buyer doesn't cancel her best retailing styles.

"So, how can you possibly cancel our best-performing styles?"

Angela stared at the computer report and couldn't meet my eye. "These styles are pretty good, but I've got several performing much better."

Angela was a lousy liar. My mother would say Angela had her lying face on. I laid the samples on the table in case she'd gone blind as well as deaf and dumb. "You cancel these orders, our sales performance will go down the drain. I'm sorry, but we can't accept this cancellation."

Angela lobbed an A-bomb. "Bunny Frank has been getting us incredible deals from your competitors on best sellers at a promotional price with no liability. They don't sell, I ship them back to the vendor."

I spun my mental Rolodex. I couldn't come up with a single competitor who would agree to such a crazy deal.

Angela circled our styles on the computer report. "You wanna match the deal? I won't cancel the goods."

When pigs sprouted wings. I pointed to the aisle of swimwear showrooms. "Mind sharing who gave you the deal of the century?"

Angela snapped, "Shop my floor and see." She stabbed her pen at the styles circled in red. "So, are you matching the deal or not?"

I shook my head no. "Sorry, we don't rent out our suits."

She shrugged. "If you won't match the deal, I'm canceling these orders."

Frustration tinged my voice. "Angela, with all due respect, the cancellation doesn't pass the sniff test. If you got such great deals with no liability, you don't have to cancel off any goods, no matter how slow your business is. Have Ernie call Rob. I can't accept this cancellation."

Angela slammed the computer report closed. "Did you forget who needs who here? Ditzy Swimwear could be one resource I can live without." She snarled, "You can talk to Rob or the man on the moon for all I care, but those orders are canceled."

Angela shoved the computer report into her messenger bag and strode out of the showroom.

I'd have to figure out something. Carefree Casuals was too big an account for us to lose. I tried all the next day to reach Angela. I left half a dozen messages but got no response. Was she too angry to return my call? I breathed a sigh of relief she didn't hang up when she finally answered the phone.

I asked for an appointment, and she said, "I don't have time to come to the mart. I've got back-to-back meetings all the rest of this week, plus I'm in the middle of inventory. If you wanna work with me, it's gonna have to be over here. The best I can do is squeeze you in on Friday at five o'clock for a half-hour. Take it or leave it."

I considered myself lucky and thanked her for the appointment.

****

Angry voices echoed loudly from the Clothing Concepts showroom as Queenie and I rounded the corner of the swimwear aisle. Naturally, incurable snoops like us, we stopped to eavesdrop. Louis and Ronnie wore a deer in the headlights as Clothing Concepts CEO Martin Decker angrily waved the Frank buying office promotional bulletin in the air. Martin thundered, "Bunny Frank didn't pull those specific styles out of her ass, set the wholesale prices, purport the terms on a guaranteed sales basis authorized by you two, and distribute this to her accounts all on her own!"

It certainly explained a lot.

Ronnie gulped. "She didn't. Bunny came into the showroom a while ago looking for some promotional goods at a killer price. She was OK with B and C styles." Ronnie pointed to the bulletin. "I gave her these at a great price, but I never agreed to those terms." Ronnie fingered the edge of the bulletin like anthrax coated the paper's surface. "I had nothing to do with this." Ronnie nervously twisted a paper clip until it broke in half. "When no orders arrived, I figured the promotion didn't go anywhere and forgot it." He snickered. "If there had been any interest, believe me, Bunny would have found a way to cut herself in for a piece of the pie like she always does."

Martin groused, "Clearly there was a lot of interest. A ton of orders came directly from the Frank office to our customer service."

Ronnie snapped, "Hey, I'm not a mind reader. Customer service never sent me a single order copy."

Next, Martin aimed his wrath at the clueless designer. "Louis, this has your name on it too. Can you explain it?"

Louis gave a jerk of his head. "I can't. I haven't had any contact with Bunny Frank since right after the ISAM party." Louis shuddered." If I'm lucky, I never will again."

Ronnie begged, "Come on, Martin. We would never do anything intentionally to hurt our company. Why would you hack off your own arm?"

Martin spat, "I can't decide which is worse—your denying it or approving this idiotic deal?"

Martin waved the computer report like a flag of surrender. "Those stores are dying with these styles." Martin ran a finger across a column. "Here's a perfect example. Carefree Casuals. Angela Wellborn was the first one screaming at customer service to take the suits back. Now the phone is ringing off the hook. And if you want to stay employed—" Martin's glare threatened to turn Ronnie into a pillar of stone. "—you'll hand-deliver the Carefree Casuals return authorization to her office today."

Ronnie pleaded, "Martin, we can't take those suits back. It's too dangerous a precedent to set."

Martin did not attempt to hide his disgust. "If we don't, we won't have a customer left. Without our credibility, we'll go out of business."

Louis whined like a cranky toddler who needed a nap. "What is it you expect us to do?"

Martin's face boiled as red as a Maine lobster. "I don't care if either of you has to marry Bunny Frank and father her children to fix this." Martin threw the bulletin on the table. "You've got till the end of the week to straighten this mess out with her or you're both fired."

The Clothing Concepts complex rattled like an earthquake had struck when Martin swept out of the showroom and slammed the door. Ronnie Schwartzman had the haunted face of a condemned man as he paced the length of the showroom. Every dog does get its day. Even one as pedigreed and pampered as Ronnie Schwartzman.

****

My usual route from the parking structure elevators to A Jolt of Java took me past the newsstand in front of the mart deli. My curiosity piqued as to why a half-dozen of my competitors were gathered around the West Coast Apparel News kiosk. I tapped Michael Rothman on the shoulder. “What’s so interesting?”

He unfolded his copy. The banner headline read:

Major Shake-up Rumored at Swimwear Giant

I bought a paper and walked into A Jolt of Java at the same time as Bunny Frank. She had a copy of the Apparel News in her hand and a cat who swallowed the canary grin plastered across her lips as she read the headline.

Chapter Ten

As usual, the yentas were yakking away like magpies. Sonia Wilson tapped the rim of her cup with a spoon to get our attention. "I might be moving to Mystical Dreamer Swimwear."

I burnt my tongue on my coffee. "I had no idea you wanted to make a change."

Joan studied Sonia over the top of her eyeglasses. "Me neither. Are you unhappy at Itsy-Bitsy?"

Sonia's voice was tinged with regret. "No, I love my job and adore my boss, but I've gone as far as I can with Itsy. It's purposely not geared for the big stores. Dave doesn't want the aggravation." Sonia smiled at me. "I want to do sales the way your dad taught it to you. Do the most amount of business in the least amount of time. Go after the big box stores. They're the future. I can't do it where I am. It's the right time for me to move on." Sonia's eyes shone with excitement. "Their HR said my retail background gave me a big advantage over the other candidates."

Sonia had overcome so much adversity. She deserved something to break her way. "When will you find out if you got the job?"

"I had the second interview yesterday morning. I'm hoping to find out sometime this afternoon." Sonia crossed her fingers and grinned. "Hopefully, tomorrow morning, coffee is on me."

****

Angela Wellborn and I nodded politely to one another as we entered A Jolt of Java together the next morning. I cautiously wished her a good morning and took it as a positive sign when Angela told me to have a nice day. With any luck, maybe I'd save the account.

I worked my way around the table distributing the group's coffees. When I handed Sonia her cup, the good vibe I had from Angela quickly disappeared. Sonia's complexion was gray as day-old oatmeal. Her red-rimmed eyes said it all.

I squeezed her arm. "What happened?"

Sonia's eyes filled. "I didn't get it."

"Did they tell you why?"

Sonia twisted her lips into a bitter smile. "My references didn't pan out."

Bunny Frank sat at a table across from us sipping a latte and reading the West Coast Apparel News. Sonia walked the short distance to Bunny's table. Bunny folded the paper and gave Sonia a shit-eating grin.

Sonia growled, "You're a miserable excuse for a human being. You couldn't bring yourself to do the right thing for once in your life. You had to lie and destroy a fabulous opportunity because you could."

Bunny drew a circle in the air and put her index finger through it. "Bullseye, Wilson." She wiggled her thumb and flashed an evil smile. "Gotcha right under here and I always will."

Sonia grabbed the latte out of Bunny's hand and poured the drink over Bunny's head. The concoction flowed slowly, like lava, down Bunny's face and meandered into her cleavage. Too stunned to react, Bunny sat still as a statue as the foam seeped from her décolletage and stained her white knit top.

Sonia crushed the empty paper cup and threw it on the table. The crowded room was silent as a tomb as all eyes swiveled to Bunny's table. Not a soul missed Sonia snarl, "I promise I'll get even with you. I will make you pay if it takes me forever." Sonia spun on her heel and stomped back to our table. She pointed to the barista's station. "Anyone for a refill? This round is on me."

Chapter Eleven

The psychedelic light shows of the police car's flashing strobe bubbles created an eerie specter as they bounced off the mart parking lot walls. A large group of the morbidly curious gathered across from the elevator bank were held back by a line of grim-faced uniformed LAPD. The area around the elevator was cordoned off with yellow crime scene tape framing Bunny's body like a museum exhibit. Bunny was in all her glory, in death as in life, hogging the spotlight, star of her own macabre show. Bunny Frank, the center of all the carnival hoopla? She would have been thrilled.

After Los Angeles County Assistant Medical Examiner Sophie Cutler took Bunny's temperature and encased Bunny's fingers in plastic bags, the doctor emerged from the elevator and walked over to LAPD homicide detective Miguel Martinez, the cop in charge. Five-foot eleven Sophie Cutler was a skinny, flat-chested, blonde, blue-eyed brilliant but nerdy scientist, and my life-long friend. I scissored my arms across my chest like I was guiding in a plane. "Hiya Snip."

At six-foot-two and all toned muscle, dark-haired and mustachioed Detective Miguel Martinez had the confident posture of an imposing man. His intelligent obsidian eyes didn't miss much. I studied the cop for his reaction. The corners of his lips twitched as Sophie waved back. He jerked his chin toward me. His tone was nothing short of incredulous. "Snip? Sophie, do you know her? She's the one who found the Vic."

Sophie said, "Oh yeah, we go way back. We've been friends since junior high biology. We made quite a scholastic tag team. She wrote my English essays, and I dissected her frog." Dr. Cutler sheepishly grinned. "It's how I got tagged with the nickname."

Martinez ping-ponged his eyes back and forth between Snip and me. "No kidding; she's a friend of yours? She's an interesting one."

The flush of embarrassment crept across the front of my neck.

The detective scratched his chin with his pen cap. "Her reaction to the death was certainly a first." He shook his head. "Simply amazing."

Sophie said, "Let me guess. You asked her a question regarding the decedent, and she broke out laughing; right?"

Martinez widened his eyes. "Yeah, exactly. How did you guess?"

Sophie pursed her lips. "We've been friends for a long time."

Martinez's eyebrows rose to his receding hairline. "As a cop, I've seen a lot of crazy things before, but this one wins the prize."

Sophie explained the inexplicable. "It's a nervous reaction. She has a fear of death, and it's a defense mechanism."

Martinez studied me like I was a new species. "She always reacts to death by laughing?"

Sophie sighed. "It takes some getting used to. She held it together during the eulogies at my Grandma Esther's memorial, but she lost it when the Rabbi chanted the prayer for the dead. I had one heck of a time explaining it to my mom. The Rabbi couldn't concentrate on the passages. He lost his place twice and had to start over. My Uncle Joey was two steps from throwing Holly out of the chapel until I held him back."

Martinez's facial expression suggested the men with the white coats should have taken me back to the sanitarium a long time ago. "When I first approached her, she was wisecracking to the Vic. Like a nut job."

I ground my teeth. This was as much fun as a pulled hamstring.

Snip shrugged. "She can't control it. It's an inherited trait. She comes by it genetically. Her grandma had the same reaction to a death."

Martinez raised his eyebrows. "I guess nothing should surprise me. This is LALA Land. She could do the comedy club rounds and make a fortune with this gig as a routine."

Martinez motioned toward the cordoned-off elevator. "Any guess on a cause of death or a time frame we can work off of yet?"

I leaned around my uniformed keeper so I could hear the answer.

"Nothing official till I get her on the table. But preliminarily, based on her temperature and rigor, I'd say the time of death was eight to ten hours ago. COD most likely suffocation."

Martinez widened his eyes. "This is a bizarre one, even for LA. She pissed someone off. The question is who."

Good luck, Dick Tracy.

Sophie motioned her crew to load the body bag into the Coroner's wagon. The crowd of looky-loos disappeared once the gruesome floorshow was over.

Martinez gave me the once-over again before he took a small notebook out of his jacket and clicked open his pen. "Pretty surprising Sophie Cutler let anyone write her English essays for her. She's the pickiest ME I've ever worked with. She must have trusted you an awful lot."

I laughed out loud. "Trust never entered into it. Merely a good tradeoff of skillsets. Dissecting a frog made me nauseous, and she was incapable of writing a decent essay."

Unfortunately, there wasn't much I could add to the initial statement I'd given him earlier. He closed his notebook and let me go to the showroom, with an instruction to stick around for an interview follow-up.

With the elevator bank cordoned off, the only way to the lobby was the stairs. As I opened the stairwell door, Martinez lifted the crime-scene tape and met his partner in front of the elevator bank. Curiosity kept my heel wedged in the door jam.

Martinez said, "There was no sign of a struggle. Either she was killed somewhere else and placed in the elevator postmortem or she was incapacitated before and was killed there."

Martinez's partner, Detective Glory Washington, was a compact fireplug with close-cropped kinky black hair, milk chocolate eyes, and smooth skin the tone of toasted almonds. Washington flexed her steepled fingers. "She had to be killed in the elevator."

Martinez scratched his chin with a bony index finger. "Or she was killed in the parking structure and placed into the elevator? The initial estimate of TOD was consistent with the mart pretty deserted. The ME should be able to tell us if she was trussed postmortem or not."

Washington mused, "Strange the way she was found with her arms out low. Like she was imploring the murderer to help her." Washington widened her eyes. "She knew the killer."

Martinez agreed. "Absolutely. This was no random attack. This was a rage killing. The killer made it crystal clear they were furious with the Vic."

Glory tapped a stubby finger against her lips. "What do you make of how she was trussed or the bikini in the mouth? And what's with the paper thing hanging out over her lip?"

Martinez gave his mustache a stroke. "It's the key to the whole case. The murderer wasn't satisfied killing the Vic. The killer was making a point. We figure out what the point is, and we'll get our killer."

Chapter Twelve

I got to the showroom and called Rob to explain why I'd been missing in action all morning. Buster and Hope were away for the day at a trunk show at the Oasis of the Desert hotel in Palm Springs. On the one hand, I didn't want to be alone, but on the other, I was grateful not to relive the horror by having to retell it to them. I was exhausted, but I didn't dare lean back in my chair and rest. I was afraid to. Would the image of Bunny Frank's corpse be embedded in my mind forever? When you know someone, their nightmare becomes yours the minute you close your eyes. I ordered lunch, but once it arrived, I didn't have much of an appetite and pushed the food around on the plate. I managed to avoid the yentas and bumbled through the rest of the day in a daze.

Detective Martinez came into the showroom late afternoon. "I appreciate your waiting for me Ms. Schlivnik. I've got some more questions. I'll try to keep this as short as I can." The detective's tone was gentle. "Ms. Schlivnik, we have no reason to consider you a suspect, but for purposes of elimination, can you tell me where you were and what you were doing the day and evening of the murder?"

My pulse danced the tango a couple of steps faster. I had to account for my time. I hadn't done anything wrong, and the question was routine. Still, this was my first police interrogation, let alone my first murder, and the question unnerved me. The cops found me next to the body. Even with Snip vouching for me, this cop didn't know me from the man on the moon. The leap to I killed Bunny and stuck around to either admire my handiwork or steer the detective in the wrong direction was an easy one to make. Cripes. Controlling the quiver in my voice proved impossible. "No-no problem. I-I was at our factory all day in meetings. My boss can verify my daytime schedule. After work, I had dinner with a friend. I drove out to Sherman Oaks in the valley. We met at seven-thirty at Carbone's on Ventura Boulevard. I can give you my friend Christine's contact information to confirm the dinner. If you need it, I've still got the credit card receipt from the restaurant." I opened my purse to get the receipt, but Martinez waved it off with a flick of his wrist. I almost fainted with relief. I measure four-foot-nine in my stockinged feet. Horizontal prison stripes cutting you in half? Quite a dandy fashion statement. Think a barbershop pole had a child with a fire hydrant.

Martinez went back a page or two in his notebook and circled a few words. "Gotham Swimwear is one of your competitors?"

"It is. Gotham is a division of a larger company. The parent company is Clothing Concepts." I pointed across the hall. "Their showroom takes up the whole side of the aisle across from us."

Martinez scratched a half-dozen lines in his notebook.

I asked, "Is there any significance to the particular style or the specific brand bikini jammed in Bunny's mouth?"

Martinez twirled the ends of his mustache. “At this stage of the investigation, we don’t have many answers. For now, we’re trying to figure out the right questions to ask.”

He opened his notebook to a blank page. “The tape Ms. Frank was trussed with? I’ve never seen one like it.”

“It’s a packing tape used to seal boxes for shipping. It has a thin string woven inside the tape for strength.”

Martinez crossed his arms over his chest. “It certainly worked on Ms. Frank. She was wrapped tight as a mummy.” The detective put his notebook aside and his dark eyes bored right into my soul. “Ms. Schlivnik, who wanted to do Ms. Frank harm?”

Are you kidding, detective? I struggled to find the words, but my brain had no control over my tongue. I blurted out, “Most of North America.”

The detective’s voice dripped sarcasm. “So, I take it Ms. Frank was not liked?”

Mr. Detective, you have no idea.

Martinez furrowed his brow. “Can you possibly narrow it some?”

“The apparel industry.”

Annoyance flashed in his eyes. I was either playing around or evading the question. “Seriously, the entire apparel industry?”

I held out a palm. “Most of the west coast apparel people.”

Martinez rewarded me with another one of his scowls. “There isn’t enough staff to interview so many people. Can’t you narrow it anymore?”

If he ever met Bunny Frank, he would never ask the question. “The LA apparel industry.”

The cop cocked a brow. “Come on, Ms. Schlivnik, give me a break.”

Martinez had no idea. “Ok, mart tenants.”

Martinez gave me a sideways glance. “If she was so universally disliked, how was she able to stay in business?”

“I didn’t say she was bad at what she did. I said she wasn’t liked. Bunny Frank was a force of nature. People tolerated Bunny and all the stunts she pulled because she made both her clients and vendors lots of money. They say money talks and BS walks. Bunny managed to do both.”

Martinez eyed me curiously. “What stunts?”

I counted them off on my fingers. “Bunny stopped at nothing to get what she wanted. She cheated, tricked, cajoled, lied, threatened, and pushed whoever she had to get her way.”

Martinez tilted his head. “Such as?”

I counted a second list on the fingers of my other hand. “She wasn’t above taking payoffs. She had no trouble shaking people down. She saw nothing wrong with stealing a competitor’s customers, personnel, or someone else’s products or ideas.”

Martinez pushed me beyond my comfort zone. “Can you give me specifics?”

I squirmed in my seat. I didn’t want to point him toward someone only because they’d had a run-in with Bunny Frank. I might as well hand the guy a mart directory and tell him to start knocking door to door. “I can tell you the stuff she pulled with my company. The rest would only be rumors and innuendos.”

Martinez poised his pen over his notebook, ready to write. "I need a starting place. A motive is a good one so let me have them all."

I whined like a toddler instructed to share her toys. "You want me to name names?"

The chill of Martinez's stare pierced my heart like an ice pick. "Yeah."

Cripes, we'd be here all month.

"Detective, you're asking an awful lot."

Martinez narrowed his eyes. Yikes, did he say if ya know what's good for ya, start singing? I gave a quick head shake to clear the cobwebs. He actually said, "If you wanna help us catch whoever did this, point me in the right direction."

Like I had any idea.

He pushed me to a place I was unwilling to go. "Come on, detective," I croaked. "I live with these people. You're putting me in one heck of a position."

He must have channeled my dad's guilt giving skills. "Doesn't every murder victim deserve justice, Ms. Schlivnik, even one as disliked as Ms. Frank?"

Once I'd talked myself hoarse and he'd likely run out of ink, Martinez stowed his notebook and pen in his jacket pocket. He rolled his shoulders and stretched. "LA has its share of crazies, but this is the weirdest case I've ever caught." Martinez grinned and two cute dimples cratered his cheeks. "The question isn't who wanted the victim dead; who didn't?"

No kidding, Colombo. Get in the boat and row.

****

I stopped at the newsstand in the mart lobby the next morning. Bunny's picture was plastered across the front pages of the Los Angeles Gazette, the West Coast

Apparel News, and Women's Apparel Journal. The banner headlines screamed the gruesome details of her murder. Somewhere out in the great beyond, Bunny Frank basked in her glory.

The mood was appropriately funereal as the yentas gathered around our usual table. Was there really something to be said in the strength of numbers? I hoped so because I sure wasn't doing too hot on my own. Remarkably, for the first ten minutes, no one uttered a word. This in itself was amazing. Normally, you couldn't get a word in edgewise with our group of yakkers. We drank our coffee and assessed one another. The sight wasn't pretty. Dark lines smudged below our eyes. Not one of us had slept a wink.

Bunny Frank certainly wouldn't have won any popularity contests, yet her death was unnerving. One of our own had been viciously murdered right under our roof. As mortality stared at us, the security concern was etched in our faces while fear for our lives gripped our hearts. If it could happen to Bunny Frank, it could happen to any one of us.

When the silence became awkward, I panned the table and joked, "Don't take this the wrong way, but you all look like warmed-over crap."

I finished telling the tale and flushed crimson when Queenie smirked, "So, tell the truth. Did you laugh?"

No reason to deny it. My reputation preceded me. "You have to ask?" Laughter had been my knee-jerk reaction the day before. But with the image of Bunny Frank's corpse seared into my memory, I wasn't laughing anymore.

Hope's red-rimmed eyes reflected anguish so palatable it sucked the air out of the room. Her eyes filled as she whispered, "Who would do such a horrible thing?"

Joan arced the perimeter of the packed coffee house. "Take your pick. Bunny didn't exactly have a legion of adoring fans."

I said, "The detective called it a rage killing and the person responsible was no stranger." There was no point in even trying to contain my grin. "He said someone familiar with her was extremely pissed at Bunny."

No kidding, Kojack.

Joan waved at the crowd again. "And this reduces the suspect pool how?"

She had me there.

I said, "The cops on TV always say to follow the money."

Queenie tapped her index finger on the tip of her nose. "Who had the most to lose?"

We all chorused, "Louis and Ronnie."

Joan counted a list of other names on her fingers. "Don't forget Michael Rothman, Angela Wellborn, and Sue Ellen Magee."

Michael Rothman a cold-blooded killer? Get real. He was a nice, cute, but clueless guy who made balloon figures for buyers. Angela Wellborn? No motive. Martin Decker ordered Ronnie Schwartzman to take back all of Angela's unsold promotional inventory. Sue Ellen Magee? If wishes were fishes. Sue Ellen hadn't murdered Bunny, but the undisputed bitch of bikinis was the one we were all secretly rooting for.

Sonia's laugh was mirthless. "Don't forget me."

The denial bubbling up died in my throat. Sonia was right. Her storied past with Bunny was certainly a problem. On its own, with a bit of massaging, it likely could have been explained away. But add pouring the latte over Bunny's head followed by a threat witnessed by a cast of hundreds right before Miss Congeniality's brutal murder, and Sonia easily jumps to the top of the suspect list.

When you throw gasoline on a fire, expect to be burned.

Chapter Thirteen

Queenie and I were in the mart parking lot at the end of the day. She said, "The weirdest thing happened after lunch. I'm on the way back to the showroom and Angela Wellborn nearly ran me over as she stomped out of Clothing Concepts mad as a wet hen. I asked what was wrong, and she said Louis stood her up for their lunch date. After a half-hour standing in front of the mart deli, Angela got tired of waiting. She went to his showroom, but he wasn't there. The receptionist had no idea where he was, so Angela went into Ronnie. Ronnie tells her she must have gotten the day wrong because Louis has a standing lunch appointment on Tuesdays and Thursdays. Angela was clueless about Louis' standing lunch dates and asked Ronnie who Louis met twice a week. Ronnie said he had no idea and when he questioned Louis, Louis refused to say." Queenie shook her head like a wet dog. "Weird, huh?"

I said, "Louis has something to hide."

We got to our cars and Queenie asked, "Where are you off to?"

"Dinner with Snip. Hopefully, she has updated information of what happened to Bunny." I dropped the top on the mustang and grinned. "Stay tuned for further developments."

****

The Cheesecake Café in Marina Del Rey has a unique menu and fantastic food, but with its cathedral ceilings and perennial crowd, it's difficult to hold a conversation without having to shout. I'd suggested a quieter eatery on the Washington Street pier with a spectacular ocean view. But Sophie Cutler was a dessertaholic from the last movie, so when her sweet-tooth needs a fix, anyplace else isn't an option.

I rolled my eyes as she scraped off a dollop of whipped cream from the gooey slice of cheesecake before she took a bite. She asked, "Problem?"

I dragged my eyes to the glop of whipped cream, and Snip gave me the middle finger salute. I asked, "Any idea yet how Bunny was killed?"

Before she answered, Snip glugged some coffee to wash down the huge forkful of cheesecake she'd shoved in her mouth. "I've still got some tests to run, and I'm waiting for the tox report to come back before I officially call it. Unofficially, the preliminary is she died of asphyxiation, but it's not clear how."

How many ways are there? I wiggled my fingers in Snip's face. "If she was suffocated, someone either put a pillow over her face or their hands around her neck and squeezed. Right?"

Snip said, "Ordinarily, the answer is yes. But there are no ligature marks or handprints on her neck. No injuries on her vertebrae consistent with strangulation."

"What does it mean?"

"It means until the tests come back, I can't tell you. Ms. Frank had drag marks on the backs of her legs and heels, so she was placed in the elevator; she didn't go in on her own." Snip flexed her arms like a bodybuilder. "Ms. Frank wasn't a petite woman to begin with, and by the time she was dragged to the elevator, in the condition she was in, she was dead weight. Whoever got her in there had to be pretty strong."

"It had to be a man?"

"Most likely."

Good news for Sonia. A vision of Ronnie Schwartzman in prison stripes darted across my mind. "The police are gonna focus on men?"

Snip answered, "I'd say yes, but I can't make any conclusions until I run the rest of the tests on the physical evidence."

Snip has always been a hopeless gossip hound. No one loves a juicy story more than her. She was gonna love this one. "I've got some dirt on Ronnie Schwartzman, the Regional Sales Manager for Gotham Swimwear. Gotham is the brand of the bikini stuffed in Bunny Frank's mouth."

Snip's face lit up like a kid opening gifts on Christmas morning. "Do tell."

"I found out Ronnie had been having an affair with Bunny. My friend Queenie caught a glimpse of the two of them with their lips glued to one another's leaving a hotel in Santa Monica not long before Bunny was killed."

Snip's smile faded. "Are you telling me this because it should eliminate him from suspicion? If you're going there, don't. Because many a murder victim was killed by a lover."

I beamed. "No, actually it implicates him. It explains a huge issue between his company and hers."

Snip took a break from shoveling the cheesecake into her piehole. "What issue?"

"Ronnie gave Bunny a promotional program for her stores with big discounts and guaranteed sale terms."

Snip put her elbow on the table and rested her chin in her palm. "What does it mean?"

"It means the stores don't sell the suits, they can send them back to the vendor and not have to pay for them."

Snip gave me you're joking bat of her eyes. "I'm no sales expert, but it sounds like a good way to lose your shirt. Do you sell your line the same way?"

I scoffed, "As if. It's never done. I bet Ronnie gave Bunny the deal of the century to get into her pants. Now with so many stores having done terrible with the promotion and want out of the inventory, Ronnie denied he made the deal and has refused to take any of the suits back."

Snip said, "Maybe he's telling the truth and didn't make the deal."

I said, "Bunny had a lot of chutzpah, but even she wasn't bold enough to offer such a killer deal without someone at Gotham approving."

"And what if she did?"

"Then she gave Gotham Swimwear a ginormous heap of trouble and someone there a pretty strong motive to kill her." My eyes widened. "What if Ronnie killed her when he found out what she did? He's a big guy. He's strong enough to do it."

Sophie narrowed her eyes. "Did you tell all this to Detective Martinez?"

"The promotional program, yes, but not the affair. I just found out yesterday. Besides, I don't wanna point fingers. Ronnie's affair with Bunny may have been nothing more than a stupid guy thinking with the wrong head."

Sophie chuckled. "Sticks and stones. You've gotta tell Martinez. Let him decide if it means anything or not."

****

The next day I had a momentary twinge of guilt for the world of hurt I'd sent Ronnie Schwartzman's way. But when I pictured the arrogant smirk perpetually plastered on his lips, I didn't feel as bad.

Some days it's not good to be king.

Chapter Fourteen

When I finished telling the story, Joan twisted her lips into a wry smile. "Now it all makes sense."

I asked, "What does?"

Joan said, "Yesterday I was in the front part of our showroom steaming samples. It gets pretty hot when I'm steaming, so I had the showroom door open to let some cool air in. Detective Martinez walked past our showroom on his way to Gotham. The aisle was stuffy and their showroom door was open too. Their voices carried. I didn't get it all, but it sounded like Martinez put Louis and Ronnie through the wringer." Joan queried the table. "The arrogant smirk? The one Ronnie always has plastered on his kisser?"

We bobbed our heads like a group of synchronized bobblehead dolls.

Joan smiled like an infant with gas. "All Ronnie had to do was say hello, and Martinez looked like he wanted to reach across the table and wipe the smirk off the jerk's face."

Take a number and get in the back of the line, detective.

Joan said, "Martinez points to the rear of the showroom, where the offices are? He asks Ronnie if there's someplace more private for them to talk? Ronnie says no; he's got nothing to hide. Right out there in the showroom is fine. Martinez says ok, suit yourself, and he gets to it." Joan closed her eyes in concentration, like she wanted to get it all right. “Martinez says something like you had a motive, the means, and the opportunity to take care of Ms. Frank.” Joan grinned. “I’m practically leaning out of the showroom by now. If the cord was long enough, I’d have wheeled the steamer into the hallway.”

Get in the boat and row. By then our coffees were forgotten and no doubt ice cold as the yentas hung on Joan’s every word.

Joan said, “Martinez says Mr. Schwartzman, I had a lengthy conversation with your boss and frankly, Mr. Decker blames you, not Ms. Frank for the situation your company is in. I’d say you had reason enough to get back at Miss Frank. I’d wanna destroy the person who got me in such deep trouble with my boss. Martinez picks a handful of styles from the sample rack. He says you had the best access to the swimsuit we found in the victim’s mouth. Not hard to get a roll of shipping tape. You got her here on the pretext to discuss the problem, you lured her into the elevator and killed her when you got to the garage. From where I sit, you’re pretty good for it.”

“Was Ronnie at least a little scared?” I shivered. “If Martinez accused me of murder, I’d have wet my pants.”

Joan snorted. “Are you kidding? Moron Ronnie’s response was an I couldn’t care any less eye roll.” Joan threw her hands in the air. “What does Ronnie do? He yawns and puts his feet on the showroom table right in the cop’s face.” Joan widened her eyes. “Ronnie joked even if he wanted to kill Bunny, he couldn’t afford to replace her.”

Queenie furrowed her brow. “What did he mean?”

A universal shrug was the response.

Joan aimed her fingers like a pistol. "Martinez managed to restrain himself and not take his gun out and shoot the jerk. He says Mr. Schwartzman, you could lose your job and your equity interest in a huge company and all the benefits of ownership. Let's not mess around anymore. Where were you the day and evening of the murder? Ronnie says he was in the showroom all day and left the mart at six. It took him an hour to get home. The kids were busy, so he took his wife to Big Mike's for chiliburgers."

I scoffed, "Burgers with his wife wasn't much of an alibi."

Joan's face lit bright as the north star. "Martinez said the same thing and finally wiped the smirk off Ronnie's kisser. Martinez lets Ronnie go, but says not to leave town. Now it's Louis Chennault's turn at-bat. Louis takes the same seat where Ronnie had sat. Martinez suggests they talk back in Louis' office and Louis says the same thing as Ronnie; he's got nothing to hide. The cop gives him the big eyes but dives in. Martinez says Mr. Chennault, you had both a personal and a professional relationship with Ms. Frank. How do you characterize those relationships?" Joan makes a face like she swallowed a lemon whole. "Louis puffed his chest out like a proud peacock and says Bunny was a royal pain in the ass but she was one fine piece of ass."

Hope closed her eyes and cringed. "He should rot in hell."

Joan said, "Martinez ignored the crass comment and asked if Louis and Bunny were still close. Louis says no, he hardly had any interaction with Bunny at all. Louis was selling but Martinez wasn't buying. Martinez says Louis had quite a bit of interaction with Bunny." Joan swatted the air. "Louis waves it off like Bunny was nothing. He says, they had a short affair a long time ago. The affair ended quickly for him but not for her. She chased him, but he wasn't interested in getting caught. Professionally, she was one of his company's many customers. He explained he was in design, not sales so they didn't do any direct business together."

Grudgingly, I had to agree.

Joan said, "Martinez hits Louis with the run-in at the ISAM party and the lunch at the Showroom, but Louis sluffed it off. Next Martinez hit Louis with the promo issue."

Queenie asked, "How did Louis spin it?"

Joan got an evil gleam in her eye. "He threw Ronnie right under the bus. Ronnie was the one who made the deal with Bunny, not him. Claimed he knew zip until Martin confronted them with the memo."

I lifted a shoulder. "He was probably telling the truth."

Sonia sniffed. "And fifty cents won't buy you a cup of coffee."

Joan turned to me. "Martinez must have agreed with you because he said it didn't matter. Even if Ronnie orchestrated the program, Louis bore the brunt of the blame. Ronnie was collateral damage. Bunny did what she did, weaponize Ronnie to destroy Louis."

Love and hate; the eternally entwined emotions ruling our lives. Would Bunny risk it all to destroy Louis? You betcha. In a Cincinnati minute.

Queenie asked, "What did Louis say?"

Joan said, "Louis snarled You. Are. Wrong. We were not close, and we had no relationship. He told Martinez he did his best to avoid her at all costs, but Bunny was not someone who took no for an answer."

No argument there.

Joan laughed like a loon. "Louis claimed he was the real victim."

What a slimeball. Louis and Ronnie deserved one another.

Joan smirked. "Martinez did mention Bunny was the real victim since she was the one who got dead. Martinez says the swimsuit stuffed in Bunny's mouth was one Louis designed. Easy to get her into the showroom if Louis was willing to give Bunny what she wanted most in life, him." Joan held out her palms. "I dunno. Louis was pretty cavalier. Martinez is telling him Bunny made it her life's work to ruin him. I'd say it's the best motive to kill her. Martinez says unless Louis had one rock-solid alibi for the day of the murder, his troubles with Bunny Frank were going to get a lot worse."

Queenie asked, "Did he?"

Joan arched a brow. "Louis certainly thought so. He was chomping at the bit to brag he was in the mountains shacked up with a nameless married woman."

Geesh, what did Bunny ever see in this guy?

Joan said, "Martinez asks for the woman's name and Louis says he doesn't kiss and tell. Martinez asks if Louis has any hotel or restaurant receipts, and the putz says they never left the mystery woman's cabin. Martinez told him if he had no proof he was in a lot of trouble. All of a sudden Joe Cool was wetting his pants."

Chapter Fifteen

I'd spent a delightful hour at Sue Ellen Magee's office while she made some rather unreasonable demands. As a reward for the restraint I exhibited by not slapping her silly, I stopped at A Jolt of Java on the way back. I paid for my cuppa and was putting my wallet back into my purse when my cell phone rang. The voice at the other end of the line was frantic. "Thank God you answered." The electric current of Sonia's panic pulsed through the phone like a lightning strike. "Detective Martinez was here." Her voice cracked, and my heart leaped to my throat. "My God, he thinks I killed Bunny!"

I jabbed the elevator button a half dozen times, but the car didn't arrive any faster. "I'm on my way."

Sonia paced like a caged tiger. I took a seat at a workstation and appraised my normally perfectly coiffed friend. Her curly mop of dirty blonde hair stood on edge like a rooster's comb plugged into an electric outlet. Black rivulets of mascara had dribbled from her cheeks into a Rorschach inkblot onto her pale pink silk blouse. She sat next to me and stared at her lap like it held the answers to her problems. She whispered so low I considered attaching my ear to her mouth. "He got an anonymous tip on the thing at A Jolt of Java."

I can't say I was surprised. When you throw gasoline on a fire, expect to be burned.

She scrubbed at the tears running down her cheeks with the heels of her hands. She wiped the dregs of her runny mascara on the back of an order pad. “Martinez had my whole life story: my divorce and all the problems I had with Bunny. At first, I tried to downplay it. Bunny wasn’t one of my biggest fans.”

Sonia pulled a shredded tissue out of her pants pocket and honked into it like a wounded goose. “He found out I’d worked for Bunny as a buyer at Hoffman’s and she had accused me of taking bribes. She forced me to resign, and when I couldn’t find another buying job, the kids and I had to move in with my folks.” Sonia took a pen and notepad off the table and doodled a hangman. “She made me a pariah in retail, and I had to start from scratch in wholesale.” She blinked with guileless eyes. “How did he get so much information on me?”

Must be why they call him the detective.

She twisted the strands of her hair into a small knot. “Bunny is still giving me grief from the grave. He claimed Bunny gave me a bad reference and it’s why I lost the Mystical Dreamer job. I admitted I got a bad reference, but when I said I couldn’t be sure it was from Bunny, he laughed in my face. He asked, Ms. Wilson, do you make it a habit of pouring a latte over someone’s head you only suspect doing you wrong?”

I hid my amusement behind my coffee cup.

Sonia’s sigh was weary. “I tried to shine it on. I let my temper get the best of me. Bunny affected a lot of people the same way.”

No argument there.

Sonia took the picture of her kids off her desk and lost her cool. "He even found out Bunny was blackmailing me."

I almost spat my coffee across the room. Bunny was blackmailing Sonia? Desperation etched lines of fear in my friend's face. Everyone has a breaking point. Did Bunny finally push Sonia beyond hers?

She choked, "Martinez found a ledger in Bunny's office files." Sonia blinked rapidly, as if she had something in her eyes. "Bunny was like a loan shark. I wasn't the only one she was blackmailing."

I scrolled through my mental Rolodex, and it pinged like a Vegas slot machine.

Sonia's frightened eyes pleaded for absolution. "I've never accepted a bribe in my life, but I had no choice; I had to pay her off. I'd lose my job and my kids if it got out I was accused of taking bribes."

She was right. Her career was toast if there was even a hint of it. The court of public opinion doesn't give any benefit of the doubt. Guilty unless proven innocent. Next case.

She gulped. "The more the cop talked, the guiltier I sounded. He counted off all the reasons Bunny gave me to do her harm." Sonia arranged and rearranged the samples on a rack to have something to do with her hands. "He said I had access to swimsuits and hangtags."

And so what? Everyone else on the aisle did too.

Sonia walked past the storage room. "The shipping tape was in the supply box. And because I work in the mart, I could easily lure Bunny over to make a payoff and kill her instead." Sonia shuddered and held out her hands. “I expected him to take out the handcuffs and slap them on my wrists.”

No kidding. It begged the question of why he didn’t?

Sonia put the photo of her children back on her desk, and her voice cracked. “What would happen to my kids? Their father can’t even manage to send them birthday cards on the right date, let alone pay his child support. He’d take them in and raise them properly?” She snorted her derision. “Not in this lifetime.” Her panic was palpable. “I don’t even have a good alibi. My kids were at a sleepover with my parents, and I was home alone reading.” She laughed a gallows laugh. “By the time the cop finished listing all he’s got on me, even I’d say I did it, but I swear I didn’t.”

The pleading in her voice tugged at my heartstrings. “Hol, you’ve gotta help me.”

I might be incurably nosy, but I’m certainly no Miss Marple. So, no one was more surprised than me when a voice sounding an awful lot like mine reassured Sonia. “You didn’t kill Bunny. I promise we’ll find who did.” I hugged my friend and feared I’d made a commitment I had no idea how to keep.

Chapter Sixteen

The moment I answered the phone, my innards twisted around like a slinky. And all Sophie Cutler did was say hello. “I have an update on the results of the toxicology reports. Ms. Frank had enough digitalis in her system to kill a whale.”

I parroted,” Digi-what?”

She repeated, “Digitalis.”

Like this told me anything? “What is it?”

“Digitalis is a drug prepared from the dried leaves of a garden variety shrub called Foxglove. It contains the notable substances dioxin and digitoxin. Digitalis has a medicinal usage. It’s commonly used to control irregular heart rhythms called arrhythmias. It also strengthens the heartbeat by stimulating the heart muscle and increasing the amount of calcium in heart cells. But used improperly, digitalis can be deadly. It can make the heart stop.”

Besides a miserable disposition, there didn’t appear anything else wrong with Bunny, but who am I to say? Could a bad ticker explain her bizarre behavior? “Bunny had a heart condition?”

Surprise laced the tone of Snip’s voice. “No; this is the odd part. Ms. Frank had no existing heart condition warranting taking this medication. She died of heart failure caused by digitalis toxicity.”

I scratched my head. “Wait a minute. Now I’m confused. At first, you said Bunny was suffocated. Now you’re saying she wasn’t?”

“She was, but not the way you’d imagine. No one put their hands around her neck and squeezed. The digitalis led to her suffocation, and heart failure was the result. By the way, the swimsuit was inserted into her mouth postmortem, and she was also trussed postmortem.”

“Postmortem as in after she was dead*?*”

“Yep, as in after she was dead.”

Eek. “If you diagnosed strangulation, why would you even consider this digitalis?”

“Before I got her on the table, I wouldn’t have. But once I got her open, digitalis toxicity was obvious. Her heart had trauma, and the body had pre-mortem swelling along with dangerously low levels of potassium and magnesium in her system. Those are all classic signs of digitalis toxicity.”

Say what? “You’re saying Bunny didn’t take the digitalis? Someone else put a big dosage into her?”

“Precisely.”

Yikes.

Snip’s tone of voice clanged like a warning bell. “Speaking of digitalis; Ms. Wilson’s a friend of yours, so I figured you ought to know. Martinez found out Ms. Wilson’s former husband is a pharmacist. The detective speculated your friend had access to digitalis from her ex.”

I scoffed, “Don’t go to the bank on it. Sonia and the ex are barely on speaking terms.”

Snip whined her complaint. “Hey, don’t shoot the messenger. Just a heads up; Martinez is trying for an arrest before rush hour.”

I choked, “Holy crap.”

She tsked. “Calm your jets, Josephine. I told Martinez not so fast. Digitalis can be ingested by several means, not necessarily taken orally by way of a pill. An injection is another way, but I didn’t find any needle marks on the body.”

Come again? “Then how did it get into her body?”

“If not in pill or injection form, the most common way is in contact with the plain old garden variety of Foxglove.”

I looked at the phone wonky. “She died from eating a poisonous part of a plant?”

Snip laughed, “No. It’s not like Ms. Frank ate a Foxglove salad for lunch. She ingested the digitalis, but in a different way. The killer likely ground the Foxglove leaves into a powder and slipped it into Ms. Frank’s drink.” Snip couldn’t soft-soap it. Bunny Frank didn’t leave this world easily. “With the amount she’d ingested, the Vic starts to feel nauseous, and the blurred sight sometimes called Yellow Vision often follows. Abdominal pain, diarrhea, headache, dizziness, and with enough of a dose, confusion, even delirium is all possible. All those symptoms would have played into the killer’s hand. The Vic was in no condition to fight. The Vic is feeling awful and gladly goes with the killer if promised help. By the time they got into the elevator, the victim is experiencing difficulty breathing. Like she was being strangled, but from within. The Vic’s heart is in distress and on its way to failure. Ms. Frank didn’t go peacefully. She suffered an awful death. If Ms. Wilson didn't get the digitalis from her ex, Martinez suggested your friend may have a green thumb. She could have picked Foxglove from her garden and given our Vic a special treat."

I ground my teeth. "For your information, Sonia Wilson lives in a high-rise apartment off of Wilshire in Westwood, south of UCLA. The plants she's got in her apartment are artificial. So, unless you can extract digitalis from a silk flower, Sonia wasn't grinding any leaves. Trust me, Sonia Wilson couldn't tell the difference between Foxglove and a foxhunt."

The inevitability in her tone twisted my heartstrings into square knots. "Unfortunately for her, Detective Martinez is Laser beamed on Sonia Wilson."

I snapped, "And I'm tellin' you she didn't do it."

"Don't get your panties in a bunch yet." Snip's sigh was tinged with the weariness of someone who always had to deliver bad news. "I held him off. I'm still waiting for the rest of the DNA cross to come back."

****

As I was leaving to meet Queenie for lunch, I got a second call from Snip, and the rest of my day instantly went right into the crapper. "Hey kiddo, it's Snip. I got the DNA and fingerprint tests back. Our perp isn't identified yet, but it is definitely a woman. If Ms. Wilson's a friend of yours, you better tell her Martinez is eyeing her pretty closely. If she's got anything to get herself off the hook, now is an excellent time for her to bring it out."

Chapter Seventeen

Buster Schumansky and I were on our way back from Sam's, the greasy spoon diner on Ninth Street across from the mart. As the elevator doors opened on the eleventh floor, Detective Martinez stood next to Sonia Wilson. She wore a petrified expression on her face and a set of handcuffs shackled to her wrists.

Martinez glared at me, but I paid him no attention. I warned her with a waggle of my index finger. "Do. Not. Say. One. Single. Word. Do you understand me?"

She nodded yes and lifted her hands to swipe at the tears on her cheeks. Buster and I switched places in the elevator with Martinez and Sonia.

I asked, "Do you have a lawyer?" She mouthed no. As the elevator door closed, my eyes locked with hers. I pointed at Martinez. "No matter what he says, don't react; don't cry, don't sigh, and if he asks you a question, no matter how innocent it sounds, don't answer. Keep your mouth shut until my Uncle Barry gets to the precinct."

Sonia blinked her understanding, but there was no recognition of my uncle's name in her eyes. No biggie. In a short time, Barry Schlivnik would become the most important man in Sonia Wilson's life. While my uncle was a Beverly Hills personal injury lawyer who never practiced criminal law, I trusted him to find the best one.

****

The second hand of the wall clock above the Rampart Division precinct reception room hadn't moved a tick since the last two times I checked. Between the traffic and construction on Olympic Boulevard, it could take my uncle days to get downtown from Beverly Hills. I'd abandoned all hope of his arrival before Sonia's conviction when Uncle Barry purposefully strode into the police station.

If I closed my eyes and listened to the flat Midwest twang and deep bass laugh rumbling like a distant clap of thunder, it would be difficult to tell my Dad apart from Uncle Barry. Along with a sharp mind, a common sense of decency, and a wicked sense of humor, was where the brothers' resemblance ended. Tall, thin, pale-skinned, athletic Uncle Barry was the physical opposite of my olive-skinned, on the short side of average, chunky father.

A gnarled gnome of an ancient gray-haired woman was at my uncle's side. She wore an expensive business suit with support hose. Despite her high-top sneakers, she struggled to keep pace with my long-legged uncle. No one calls either Queenie or me tall, but compared to this miniature-sized woman, we were a couple of basketball centers. Who the heck was she? Heather, my uncle's perky secretary, was five decades younger and a foot taller than the gnome. Who was the old crone? A paralegal? Where the heck was the other lawyer? I checked, but nobody else was behind my uncle and his tiny companion. Was there another attorney, or had my uncle branched out into criminal law?

With surprising strength, considering her age and the size of it, the old woman smacked an overstuffed leather briefcase ready to explode on the security table with a loud thunk. She announced herself to the desk sergeant, who smiled his recognition as he examined the contents of the briefcase. He handed it back to her, and she hauled herself onto one of the uncomfortably hard plastic chairs across from us in the waiting area.

The gnome's gravelly voice sounded like she'd gargled with razor blades most of her life. "You the one with all the tsuris?" I couldn't swear I got it right. Her dentures shifted when she pronounced her vowels and garbled her speech.

I caught the amused expression in Uncle Barry's eyes. He waved a hand at the old lady and to my utter astonishment, announced, "Holly, I'd like you to meet Rose Markowitz, criminal attorney at law."

I shifted my eyes discreetly over to Uncle Barry. Was he kidding? Who was her first client? Jesus Christ before the Romans nailed him to the cross? Uncle Barry ignored my daggers and smiled into the gnome's watery blue eyes. His voice had a touch of reverence. "If I was ever in trouble with the law, Rose Markowitz is the one attorney I would call." Sincerity shined in Uncle Barry's eyes. With a leap of faith and complete trust in my uncle, I put Sonia Wilson's life in Ms. Markowitz's hands.

I pointed to the security door. "No, I'm her friend. The one with the tsuris is in there." For those who don't speak much Yiddish, tsuris roughly translated means trouble.

The gnome tapped an arthritic finger to her bony chest and grinned a toothy smile. "Don't worry, dahling. I'm on the case now. It's all gonna be fine." Ms. Markowitz perched a pair of oversized readers on the tip of her hooked nose. She held out a scratchy hand-written note on a post-it an arms-length away. "Client's first name is Sonia?" When I answered yes, she batted a wink. "Good, good. My mother, she should rest in peace, was also named Sonia. With any luck, I'll remember the client's name."

There was a ringing endorsement. Uncle Barry shrugged, but there was laughter in his eyes. The security door creaked open, and Rose Markowitz launched herself out of the plastic chair like a rocket when Detective Martinez walked out. He recognized Ms. Markowitz and bent in half to shake her hand. He paled when he realized Ms. Markowitz, not Uncle Barry, was representing Sonia Wilson.

Ms. Markowitz hefted the strap of the huge briefcase over her narrow shoulder and tugged on the detective's jacket sleeve. "Come on Mickey, I've got an innocent client in there you're giving a lot of tsuris. I'll need some time alone with her." The gnome clucked her tongue with disapproval. "When I'm finished talking to my client, you and I will straighten out all this nonsense."

The diminutive dynamo swung back to Uncle Barry and me as an afterthought. "Why don't you two go get a cuppa coffee?" She waved a blue-veined hand with arthritic knuckles swollen to the size of golf balls toward the precinct exit. "This may take a while." She jutted her chin at a chastened Detective Martinez. "Mickey here's a gotta lot of 'splaining to do."

****

After thanking my uncle and Ms. Markowitz for helping my friend, I said my good-byes and headed for the beach. I met Queenie for dinner at Pasta at the Pier, a locals Marina del Rey eatery two blocks east of where

Washington Street dead-ends into the beach. I was a third of the way through my Sonia story when Queenie waved her half-empty glass of scotch at Mario, the restaurant owner. “Something tells me I’m gonna need a lot more shots.”

Better yet, tell Mario to leave the bottle. You’re gonna need it.

I had Queenie in hysterics when I described Ms. Markowitz, but the seriousness of Sonia Wilson’s situation was sobering. I finished the story, and Queenie lasered me with an incredulous glare. “So, you’re saying Sonia is still in jail?”

I smiled tightly. “I’ve been assured she’ll be out soon but for the moment, regrettably yes.”

Queenie was having none of it. “Why is she still in jail if this midget lawyer is supposed to be so good?”

I trusted Uncle Barry’s judgment, but still, the question begged an answer. I squirmed in my seat. “It’s complicated.”

Queenie’s tone was apologetic. “Your uncle is no slouch, so I’m not saying his opinion of this lawyer is off, but still...”

I finished her sentence. “But Sonia’s still sitting in jail.”

Queenie banged her fist, and the dregs of her scotch sloshed onto the checkered tablecloth. “We can’t sit around and wait for some old crone to get Sonia outta this mess. We’ve gotta do something, but what?”

I shrugged. “Find the real killer.”

Chapter Eighteen

Word of Sonia Wilson's arrest raced through the mart with the speed of a wildfire. The next morning the yentas stared at Sonia's empty seat and mourned as though it was her gravestone. If we didn't do something fast, it might be fait compli. Each of us brought something special to the yentas. Tenacious Sonia was the heart of the group who taught the rest of us how to face any challenge with courage and grace.

Joan growled like a junkyard dog. "This is a crock. She's being railroaded. It's a bunch of circumstantial BS. Why focus on her and nobody else?"

Hope asked, "Such as?"

Queenie didn't hesitate. "Michael Rothman. Maybe he got tired of paying Bunny's extortion."

My hands fluttered the air. "It's probably a longshot. Martinez is focusing on women."

Joan piped, "Sue Ellen Magee's got my vote."

Queenie snorted, "If Sue Ellen Magee stuffed a bikini in Bunny's mouth, she would have signed her name to the hangtag."

She had us there.

Queenie said, "Besides, Sue Ellen had no motive. Sue Ellen didn't buy the Gotham promo, and she dodged the working for Bunny rumor. Sue Ellen didn't get promoted, but she still has her job. She might want to, but she wouldn't murder Bunny for pulling a stupid stunt."

Queenie was right, but it's a darned shame. Sue Ellen Magee in horizontal prison stripes? Her ample, apple-shaped ass would resemble the broad side of a barn. There was a vision. Yeah, it is pretty catty. Too bad. Meow.

Joan tossed out a worthy candidate. "Angela Wellborn. There's a mountain of unsold promos dying on her floor."

I've been on Angela's floor. Joan wasn't whistling Dixie.

Queenie shook off the suggestion. "She would have been my favorite choice too except Angela's got no motive either. Martin directed Ronnie to take back all her unsold suits."

I held out my palms like a rush-hour traffic cop at Times Square. "Hold on a minute. It still might be her. Maybe Ronnie isn't too good at following orders."

Hope asked, "Any other women?"

Joan stood and faced the exit. "Don't go away. Let me dash to the showroom and get the mart directory so we don't miss any."

Hope sighed with defeat. "If the killer is a woman, we eliminated the two most obvious ones." She snapped her fingers. "Wait a darned minute. We forgot the buyers at the other buying offices."

Queenie dismissed the idea with a flick of her wrist. "Nah. It's true Bunny played it loosey goosy with the way she conducted her business, but even if it's dirty pool, competition doesn't get you killed."

Who says so?

"I dunno; at the ISAM party, Ellen Thomas was ready to kill Bunny Frank." I dipped my head. "And don't discount Leticia Lapidus from the Atlas office. I was next to Bunny and Leticia in the mart stationery store when Leticia accused Bunny of stealing one of the Atlas graphic artists. Bunny admitted it and Leticia threatened to kick Bunny's ass if she poached any more Atlas staff."

Joan blew out her cheeks. "We've gone to Cleveland by way of Cairo and we're still nowhere." She puckered her lips like a funnel. "Do we just sit around like bumps on a log and pray the midget lawyer springs Sonia?"

I said, "Not a chance. Martinez has already made up his mind Sonia did it. He isn't gonna put any effort into investigating anyone else. If we want the real killer caught, we're gonna have to do the detective's heavy lifting for him. The case against Sonia doesn't pass the sniff test." I smiled at my friends. "Stay tuned. I've got an idea but I'm not ready to share it." I toasted the empty chair with my coffee cup. "Hang in there, princess. The cavalry is coming."

Time to saddle up.

****

Queenie and I shopped stores hoping to get our minds off Bunny's murder, but it wasn't to be. Reminders followed us like a shadow. The Carefree Casuals swimwear department was more like a Gotham Swimwear company store. While we shopped, I laid out my idea. Remarkably, Queenie didn't have me committed. In retrospect, she probably should have.

We left the Century City Mall as it closed and drove back to the mart. Once we got past the eleventh-floor elevator bank, dim security lights provided little illumination. We crept along the pitch-black hallway to the swimwear aisle and felt our way like a couple of blind mice. We craned our necks around like submarine periscopes the length of the aisle. The good news? No one else on the aisle was working late. The bad news? I couldn't find my finger in front of my nose.

Burgling Ronnie's showroom was a great idea as an idea. But I hadn't worked the actual details out. The Clothing Concepts showroom was enormous. It spanned the entire west side of our aisle. An industrial-sized master lock guarded the showroom door. Fantfreakingtastic. We might as well burgle Fort Knox.

I joked, "Are your lock picking skills any good? Breaking and entering aren't exactly my strong suits."

Queenie said, "We're not gonna break-in. We've got Ronnie's spare key."

Most of the swimwear vendors on the eleventh floor had been in the same showrooms for years. We were friendly competitors who kept an eye out for one another. Exchanging showroom keys with your neighbor was a common practice. Mental head slap. Sonia Wilson and I had done the same thing.

Queenie found the keyhole and unlocked her showroom door. When she flipped the master light switch on, the entire aisle lit like a lighthouse beacon. She giggled like a naughty schoolgirl and killed the showroom lights. "Oops, the whole world doesn't need to be in on this little adventure."

Queenie switched the backlights on, and I followed her into Joan's office. She rooted around on top of Joan's desk, but no keys were laying on it. Queenie jiggled the handle on the center drawer. "Cross your fingers Joanie doesn't lock her desk. If she does, we're screwed." She pulled the drawer open and grabbed a key fob labeled Clothing Concepts. She waved it as triumphantly as though it was a pot of gold. "I hold the keys to the castle."

Gulp. My stomach dropped to my toes. Now that we were going to do it, maybe the great idea wasn't such a great idea after all. "We're gonna find proof Ronnie killed Bunny? Even if he was dumb enough to leave anything incriminating around, does a prima donna like Ronnie Schwartzman get his hands dirty?"

Queenie smiled. "Only one way to find out."

I trailed behind her back into the Royal showroom. "Martinez already searched the place. Whatever evidence there was, he must have already taken out."

Queenie's glare could have shattered glass. "Now this revelation occurs to you?" She wrinkled her nose like she smelled a fart. "How would Martinez even realize the evidence is the evidence?"

Like we would? "They must teach those kinds of things in detective school."

Queenie rolled her eyes. She switched off the lights and locked her showroom. I followed behind like an obedient baby duckling as she crossed the aisle. Queenie clicked the Clothing Concepts padlock open with one clockwise twist. "Your pal the coroner thinks Bunny was killed by a woman, but she could be wrong." Queenie pushed the door open and waved me in. "Come on, Nancy Drew. Bunny had a legion of enemies, but Louis and Ronnie are still the ones who had the most to lose. Let's go prove it."

We opened the beveled double doors of Ronnie's huge executive office, and my jaw dropped. This wasn't an office; this was a palace fit for a king. Ronnie's office was half the size of my showroom. A mahogany desk the size of an aircraft carrier sat in the middle of the room on a hand laid peg and groove wooden floor. A top of the line computer and Tiffany desk lamp centered a large leather-bound blotter next to the six-line phone. The high back soft as butter leather desk chair was more like a throne. On a wall across from the desk were a grid and a rack with a sample line hung on it. The shelves of the credenza to the right of the desk were filled with bound computer reports. Two file cabinets were stationed like sentries on opposite sides of a mirrored closet behind the desk.

To the left of the desk was a conversation corner with a sofa, a love seat, and coffee table all set on a Persian area rug. A bar in the opposite corner had a coffee maker on top. A bar-sized mini-refrigerator and a liquor cabinet sat behind it. A flat-screen TV and stereo system were suspended from the ceiling. The office had a full bathroom with a stall shower, a jacuzzi tub, along with the toilet and sink.

I joked. "If Ronnie's wife ever throws him out, he can live here."

Queenie walked around the room in awe. "Are you kidding? I'd ditch my condo and move in here yesterday. It's like we're burgling the Taj Mahal."

What wouldn't Ronnie Schwartzman do to protect all this? My guess was there's nothing he wouldn't do.

Chapter Nineteen

I checked the time and got nervous. Our office tour had taken way too long. "Let's get to it."

Queenie wrinkled her nose. "What are we looking for?"

I sucked in my cheeks. "Not exactly sure. Guess we'll know it when we see it?"

"How do ya wanna do it?"

Like I had any idea.

Queenie pointed across the hall. "Do you want to take Ronnie's office and I'll take Louis'?"

I shook my head no. "Nah, we'll get done faster if we go through each office together."

Queenie agreed, "You're right. Two sets of eyes are better than one. We can't afford to miss anything because we've got one shot at this."

No kidding. The way my heart was pounding, I'd never make it through an encore performance. "I'll take the desk. You take the credenza, and when we're done, we'll go through the closet and the files."

Ronnie was a big guy, over a foot taller than me. Naturally, the adjustment level of his chair was raised for his height. I took five steps back and launched myself into the chair like a long-jumper and sank into the plush cushioned seat up to my neck. When I sat back, my feet didn't come close to reaching the ground. I wiggled my ass around trying to get some traction. Cripes, if Queenie wasn't there to pull me out, I could be stuck in this thing all night. Still, the leather was soft as a marshmallow, and a girl could get used to this.

I opened the center drawer first. Besides a pack of condoms, a stick of sugarless gum, two quarters, an eyeglass case, two fancy fountain pens, a mechanical pencil, several keys on a ring, and a complicated-looking calculator capable of figuring a rocket's fuel consumption, there was nothing of any significance.

The left-side desk drawer was half open and Queenie whispered, "You hear anything?"

I whispered back. "No. Why?"

Queenie raised her voice half an octave. "I could have sworn the showroom door opened."

Cripes. I strained my ears, but aside from my pulse ticking like a time-bomb, I didn't hear a sound. "You've gotta be kidding."

Queenie put a shushing finger to her lips. "I wish I was." She crept to the office door and put her ear against it. Two minutes later she shrugged and went back to the credenza. "Guess I'm imagining things."

I tapped my fingers against my chest to restart my heart. "Thank God. How could we ever explain our being here?" How indeed.

I tackled the drawer on the left side of the desk. It held line lists, color brochures, and a stack of thick files of Ronnie's biggest accounts. So far, the desk was a big nothingburger. I pulled on the handle of the right drawer, but it wouldn't budge. I took the keyring out of the center drawer and tried all the keys, but none of them worked. I jimmied the lock with a paperclip three times and no go. Better keep my day job. My lock picking skills could use some practice.

Maybe the drawer wasn't locked. It might be stuck. I yanked on it, but it wouldn't open even an inch.

Queenie said, "Hol, I'm going crazy."

"Why?"

"I swear there is a voice out there."

Fingers of panic twisted my heart. My God. Ronnie? If he caught us, he'd have our heads on a platter. I squeaked like a mouse. "Whose voice? Ronnie Schwartzman's?"

She laughed, "Not unless his voice is forty octaves higher and he's talking in Spanish." Queenie whispered, "You don't hear anyone talking?"

I strained my ears. Nothing but the sound of my pulse pounding. "Nope. But let's find whatever we're gonna find and get outta here all the same."

I rooted around the middle drawer, but there was nothing useful, like a nail file, to jimmy the lock. I was out of options. For giggles and squeaks, I opened the eyeglass case. Behind the glasses was a hundred-dollar bill tucked into an oddly-folded chamois cleaning cloth. When I unfolded it, a small gold key fell out of the C-note. I twisted the key counterclockwise and the drawer lock clicked open. Bingo. Bongo. Jackpot. I laid a small ledger on the desk. I squealed like a stuck pig. "Come over here, I've got something."

Queenie leaned over my shoulder as I opened the ledger. Each page had a series of columns marked with a weekly date, a cash entry, and the initials BF next to the amount. The amounts were enormous. If I was reading the ledger correctly, Ronnie Schwartzman had been paying Bunny Frank $5,000.00 a week in cold cash for the last two years. I circled the final entries with my finger. "The last two weeks before Bunny was killed, Ronnie paid her an additional $10,000.00 per week. Those had to be payoffs for the promos."

I was no math whiz, but you didn't have to be Albert Einstein to figure Ronnie had paid Bunny over a half-million dollars in cash the last two years. The ledger entries didn't go any farther back. Was he paying her for a lot longer? He could have been, but there was no way to tell. Regardless of the length of time, it begged the question of why Bunny was on Ronnie's payroll at all? Unfortunately, the ledger did not detail what Ronnie was getting in return for his money. Either hush money to buy Bunny's silence or payola to buy Bunny's business. Toss a coin.

I flipped the pages back and forth. "Suppose Bunny wasn't holding up her end of the deal, and Ronnie got tired of paying? Say he took her off his payroll and she threatened to expose their agreement, whatever the deal might have been?"

Queenie pointed to the last payments. "Or if she was blackmailing him, she upped the ante, and those two mega payments were the last straws to break the camel's back."

I tapped the first page of the ledger with my index finger. "What if we've been looking at this from the wrong angle? Maybe he killed her, but it had nothing to do with the promo situation. Was their affair going on for a long time?"

Queenie tapped the tip of her nose. "No idea, but why not? Because we found out recently doesn't mean it hasn't been going on for years."

I pulled the packet of condoms out of the desk drawer, and Queenie made a face like she'd swallowed a lemon wedge whole. I said, "Maybe all those payments were hush money or he'd ended it and she was blackmailing him over their affair. What if the payment schedule was too difficult to keep pace with and he stopped? Bunny threatened to expose the affair, so he kills her to shut her up. In a nasty divorce, Ronnie's wife gets a sharp lawyer and takes him to the cleaners. Chances are he'd be wiped out."

Queenie joked, "So Bunny's murder was a financial decision?"

I shrugged. "Yeah; why not?" I could easily see Ronnie Schwartzman crunching the numbers. "California is a community property state. Whether he paid Bunny off or knocked her off, either is still cheaper than risking an expensive divorce. I've met Ronnie's wife. Rhoda's a nasty one. She'd leave him a pauper." I tapped the ledger. "Remember what the cops on TV always say? Follow the money." A copier was next to the file cabinets. "He's got a Xerox. I'll copy the ledger while you finish going over the stuff on the credenza. When you're done, start going through the file cabinets." As I leaned over the copier to press the on button, a cart rolled across the hallway and squeaked to a stop outside Ronnie's door. Two female voices were speaking Spanish, but their conversation was soon drowned out by the whir of a vacuum cleaner.

The door handle jiggled, and Queenie went white as a ghost. "Holy Crap. We forgot the cleaning crew."

I hadn't forgotten them. The cleaning crew never entered my mind.

Queenie pointed to the leg space under the massive desk. "It'll be a tight squeeze, but we can probably both fit under there."

Not a chance. The two of us were small, but it would never happen. Even if we could, Queenie's sky-high stilettos would either stick out and trip the janitor or she'd pull her feet in and stab me with one of her ice pick-thin heels. "Yeah, no problem. If you don't mind not breathing." I opened the closet door behind Ronnie's desk. "Kill the lights and come on." I grabbed the ledger and the key and closed the desk drawer. We dove into the closet and shoved Ronnie's golf bag and the rest of his crap to the back to make room. We closed the closet door as the janitor pushed the cleaning cart into Ronnie's office.

Chapter Twenty

We huddled in the dark closet for twenty minutes; it just seemed like a lifetime. When the cart squeaked out of the office, I cracked open the closet door to check the all-clear. Logic dictated getting out while the getting was good, but we'd already gone this far, so we threw logic out the window. I copied the ledger and locked it back in the drawer. I inventoried the samples on Ronnie's rack by comparing the style numbers to a line list I'd found in his drawer. Only one sample was missing on the rack. The size ten style stuffed down Bunny Frank's throat. Cripes.

We made a second sweep through the closet, the credenza, and desk drawers and didn't find a smoking gun. I gave Ronnie's office a final once-over and double-checked we'd put everything back exactly as we'd found it. With any luck, the Xerox cooled off before morning.

Had we missed anything? No clue. A game-changer might have been staring us in the face, but we didn't recognize it. No time to dwell on the what-ifs or the maybes. We barely had time to focus on what we had. I grabbed the ledger copies, killed the lights, and closed the office door.

We walked across the hall to Louis' office. I tapped my watch. "Fifteen minutes tops. We've gotta get outta here."

"Absolutely." Queenie shivered. "This was way too close for comfort."

Louis' long, narrow office was well-appointed but not nearly as opulent as Ronnie's. The back wall held a grid and a rack filled with samples. The wall opposite his desk on the right was a pictorial history of the company's products. The wall on the left had a series of black and white action photos with Louis Chennault behind the wheel of a formula one race car.

I took Louis' desk and Queenie commandeered his portfolios. The desk was an ultra-modern Lucite with chrome-trimmed clear drawers. A computer and a three-line phone were the only items on the desk. A leather and chrome-trimmed chair was pushed in behind the desk. The bottom right drawer held a dozen color tab books missing most of the tabs.

The middle drawer had four sets of colored pencils and several blank sketchbooks. The top drawer on the right held a set of plastic containers divided into sections identified by color. Inside the containers were fabric swatches matching the color labels. The top drawer on the left was filled with international fashion magazines. Most of the photos were cut out as if Louis had been playing paper dolls.

"Come over here a sec." Queenie waved a sketchbook she'd taken out of a portfolio. "Take a look at this. Something isn't right."

I looked at the sketchbook but nothing jumped out at me. "A series of group sketches. What am I missing?"

Queenie laid the sketchbook flat on the credenza so we were standing directly over the sketches. "Now?"

I bent over the sketches and squinted. "Sorry, nada."

Queenie gave me the big eyes. "Honestly?"

I gave her the big eyes right back. "Yeah, honestly. Before anyone else walks in on us, can ya show stupid me what's got your panties in such a bunch?"

Queenie tittered, "Amazing you don't see it but ok…" She lifted the sketchbook and ran her index finger around the drawings. "See how blurred and uneven they are."

I squinted. "Are they copies? Sometimes copiers blur multi-colors, especially bright ones. Why?"

Queenie took my finger and ran it over the sketches.

"These are traced. They're not originals."

Queenie gave me a high five. "Bingo."

"What does it mean?"

Queenie thumbed through the rest of the book. "It means Louis is not doing his own sketches. They're all traced."

I shrugged. "What's the big deal?"

"Louis isn't doing his own designing."

I shook my head. "Not necessarily true. Not all designers are sketchers. A lot of the ones right out of school design by doing CADS on the computer. It's the way our designer does the line. Maybe Louis designs the same way."

Queenie shook her head. "Not Louis. He's old school." She tapped the pile of sketchbooks on the credenza. "All the sketchbooks are filled. Someone is doing the sketching, but it's not him."

She had me there.

Queenie opened the door separating Louis' office from his assistant and the design studio. "Come on, let's take a quick peek."

A big stack of clippings from the European magazines sat on assistant designer Carrie Le Beau's desk. A note from Louis instructing Carrie to knock them off was clipped to the first photo. Queenie took three groups of sketches from the design table with a color key on the bottom of the page. "What's this?"

I fanned out the sketch groups and held the color chart next to them. "It's a color key. The designer uses it to tell the printer which colors go where when they cut the screens."

Queenie tapped the sketchbook. "Or it's a color key someone who is colorblind uses to remember the way styles were to be colored."

Had Louis lost his mind? "Who hires a colorblind assistant designer?"

"You've got it backward. Carrie's not colorblind. Louis is."

The proverbial lightbulb blinked on. "It certainly explains the stuff I found in his desk drawers."

We walked back to Louis' office, and I pulled out the cut-up fashion magazines. "He cut out the styles he wanted in his line from these European magazines. Those are the ones in the design studio. Carrie labeled the box with the color swatches for him."

Queenie's smile was twisted. "Their whole line has been copied from those European designs. Compare the sketches to the photos. All Carrie is doing is tweaking the colors and styling a bit for the domestic market."

I slapped my cheek. “Holy guacamole. Louis Chennault is a fraud. Can you imagine if it ever got out in the market?”

Queenie gasped. “A nuclear disaster. If buyers had a sniff Clothing Concepts was merely a fancier version of a cheap knock- off house, the company’s high prices are history. Buyers can get recycled styling from China at half the price any day of the week.”

I reasoned, “Copying is a part of the business. We all knock things off once in a while. But of all the upscale lines in the market, Gotham has always touted itself as a cutting-edge fashion-forward designer line. This ever got out, the division is history. Gotham is their signature line, so a scandal this big could tank the whole Clothing Concepts company.”

Queenie’s eyes widened. “Do Ronnie or Martin have any idea?”

“Not a chance. If they did, Louis is out on his ass.” I patted my cheeks. “Can you imagine the fortune Louis must be paying Carrie to keep her mouth shut?”

Queenie’s eyes were as big as silver dollars. “A bucket of bucks unless he’s got something huge to hold over her. There isn’t a legitimate designer who’d willingly do all the work and let someone else get all the credit.” Queenie frowned. “What does this have to do with Bunny?”

I shrugged. “Dunno. Maybe nothing. But what if Bunny had Louis’ number? Extortion wasn’t beneath her. She could have been blackmailing him or threatening to expose him.”

How high a price would Louis pay to hold onto this cushy gig? One could only imagine. I checked the time.

We still had five minutes. "I've got one last drawer to go through. Maybe the answer's in there."

Queenie went back to the credenza and I opened the last drawer. Unlike the clear Lucite drawers, the bottom left one was encased in chrome. Hidden beneath a dozen auto racing magazines was a leather envelope-shaped attaché with the initials LSC stenciled in gold above the clasp.

The attaché held two documents. I pulled them out and spread them on top of the desk. My voice caught with excitement. "Queenie, get over here. This is unbelievable."

The first one was an ornate cream-colored oversized envelope with Louis Stanley Chennault scribed in calligraphy on the front. Inside was a beautiful handwritten wedding invitation announcing the marriage of Louis Chennault to Bernice Frank.

The wedding date was the day after Bunny was murdered. I shivered as a wisp of cold air blew over the invitation. Bunny's presence loomed somewhere above the room. Clipped to the back of the envelope was a handwritten letter addressed to Louis from Bunny written on Frank of California stationery dated a week to the day before Bunny's death.

My dearest darling Louis,

Please open the envelope and find your invitation to our wedding ceremony. I always wanted a big, splashy wedding as all young girls dream of, but who needs a crowd when a quiet ceremony with us two is what's important?

Oh, Louis, I realize a week from now is such a short time, but it feels like an eternity. I can hardly wait to make you mine, all mine, forever. But in case my undying love for you alone isn't sufficient motivation for you to show up at City Hall, remember Louis; I told you when I proposed, you're gonna be mine one way or the other.

If you know what's good for you, you'll show up on time with matching wedding bands, a corsage for me, and a smile on your face. If you don't, I'm going to bring you a world of trouble. Regrettably, the promo program didn't do the trick, but I know where all the bodies are buried, and I won't hesitate to dig every one of them up. If you don't want Martin Decker, Ronnie Schwartzman, and the entire swimwear industry to find out you're a colorblind, talentless fraud who can't design an original style or sketch his way out of a paper bag, I'd start practicing I do and find a way to mean it. You're a smart man, Louis. Do the smart thing.

Till our date with destiny, I remain always, the devoted love of your life,

Your Bunny

Was she crazy like a fox or had Bunny Frank been certifiably crazy?

I fanned the air with Bunny's letter and Ronnie's ledger. "No wonder those two didn't want Detective Martinez snooping around back here."

I cocked a brow. "What if they killed her together?"

Queenie clapped and laughed. "If they didn't, why didn't they?"

Chapter Twenty-One

The next morning Queenie and I left the Rampart Division police station shaken. We'd spent a frustrating hour with the detective. Martinez scoffed at Bunny's letter and skimmed the first page of Ronnie's ledger. The only thing he was interested in was how we got the documents. He didn't appreciate my reply. "Oh, like you, Detective, we've got our ways."

Queenie asked, "What are you gonna do with the information?"

Martinez shrugged his disinterest. "The ledger doesn't indicate what the payments were for. Unless he's using it for something illegal, the way Mr. Schwartzman spends his money is no concern of mine." Martinez smiled like a shark. "Could be legit. What if he borrowed a ton of money from Ms. Frank and payback time had come?"

The suggestion was so preposterous it could have been funny. "Detective, Ronnie Schwartzman is loaded. He could buy and sell anyone on the swimwear aisle out of petty cash. I can assure you, he didn't borrow money from Bunny Frank or anyone else. Take another look at him. He had the motive and the means. Ronnie Schwartzman's daughter has a garden in their back yard. Maybe she planted Foxglove. Isn't it possible Ronnie ground the Foxglove leaves and spiked Bunny's drink?"

Martinez spoke through clenched teeth. "There was no physical evidence at the crime scene linking Mr. Schwartzman to Ms. Frank's murder. Without it, there's no probable cause. We'd never get a judge to issue a search warrant. Even if we did, and there was an acre of Foxglove growing in his yard, so what? There's no way we could prove the Foxglove in the Schwartzman garden produced the digitalis Ms. Frank died from."

Martinez fingered the copy of Bunny's letter and laughed. "This proves nothing except Ms. Frank was a couple of tacos short of a combination. We'll check it all out, but it's not going to go anywhere."

What would it take for Martinez to suspect someone besides Sonia Wilson?

Queenie barked like a junkyard dog. "Why not?" I put a warning hand on Queenie's shoulder before she took a swing at Detective Martinez.

Martinez gave her the same pitying stare he would a slow-witted child. "The right suspect is already in custody. I'm waiting for her fingerprint and DNA tests to come back so the DA can go before the grand jury and get an indictment."

Martinez opened his office door to indicate the meeting was over. "I appreciate your coming in and sharing, but you ladies need to run along. I've got an indictment to prepare for."

Should I let Queenie slug him? Tempting, but no. Instead, I asked, "Can we see Sonia?"

Martinez frowned. "I'm afraid not. You're not her lawyer."

I whined like a kindergartener. "Come on, Detective, where's your compassion? What's the harm in giving us five minutes?"

Queenie stomped her foot like an impatient toddler. "Whatssamatta? Worried we're gonna spring her?"

Martinez sneered, "Be there early to get a seat in the gallery and you can see her at the trial." The policeman's dark eyes hardened like diamonds. "Leave the detecting to the professionals. Don't interfere with my investigation again, or you'll find yourselves in the cell next to Ms. Wilson."

****

We had nothing to show for our efforts but a patronizing lecture and a not so veiled threat. Queenie slammed the car door so hard, it's a miracle it didn't come off its hinges. Good thing she wasn't the one driving. Pity a slow driver who got in this pissed-off woman's way. It wouldn't be pretty. Think road rage on steroids. "Martinez has got some nerve."

I agreed. "This was pretty unbelievable."

Queenie growled like a grizzly. "We practically deliver the two culprits on a silver platter to the cop and he spits in our eyes. What more does the guy need?"

"Apparently, a lot more persuasion."

Queenie sputtered, "And how, pray tell, do you suggest we do it? We scoured those offices from top to bottom. We already found whatever there was to be found, and the detective blew us off." Queenie warned me with a shake of her fist. "And you can forget burgling their houses or cars." She tapped her fingers on her chest. "My heart hasn't recovered from last night. There's no place left. Short of a strip search, there's nothing else we can do."

I gave her a sly grin. "There is someplace else. I'll give you three guesses, but I betcha can't get it in a million years."

Queenie snapped, “Don’t make me hurt you.”

I groused, “You take all the fun out of things.”

She gave me a sideways glance. “This is your idea of fun?”

I rolled my eyes.

Her glare was hot enough to melt a glacier. “I’m in no mood for fun and games. I had my fill with detective Martinez, so out with it.”

I sighed, “Fine, miss killjoy, have it your way. Ronnie’s got a boat.”

From her blank stare, I was speaking Swahili. “A boat?”

“Yeah, a boat. A floating vessel. You use one to travel on water. A boat.”

She parroted, “A boat.”

I waggled my fingers like I was making waves. “Like when you wanna get where you’re going a lot faster and a lot dryer than if ya had to swim. A boat.”

She snapped like a cranky turtle. “I know what a boat is, smartass. Who cares if he has one?”

“We do.”

“Why?”

“Because he’s got a huge one moored in Porto Paloma marina two basins from my houseboat.”

She sighed with exasperation. “And?”

I eyed the distance between us. Lucky for her, my arms were too short to reach across and smack her upside her head. I gritted my teeth. “And he’s a weekend boater. We go on a weeknight. We wait till dark and maybe we’ll get lucky.”

“When do you want to go?”

“Tuesday is a moonless night.”

She screwed up her face like she was in pain.

I snarked, “What’s with the face? You got a cramp or something?”

She folded her arms across her chest. “Do you get all your useless information from the farmer’s almanac or do you just pull it out of your ass?”

I sniffed. “It’s not useless information, miss smarty-pants. If you were a boater, you’d find it important for navigation. Read the Argonaut, it gives boaters all kinds of information.”

Queenie scoffed, “I’m not a boater, so who cares? And if I was, it’s a lot easier to use one of those navigation thingies. Who needs the moon and the stars? You press a button, and the thingamajig tells you which way to go.”

I tapped the steering wheel. “Mark your calendar and save the date. Tuesday night’s the night.”

Chapter Twenty-Two

Buster Schumansky and his wife LAPD homicide detective Akura Jane, "AJ" Yakamura lived in Santa Monica five blocks from the beach in a restored 1920's bungalow.

I rapped the brass knocker on their front door. "It's open," AJ's disembodied voice called out from the backyard. I could have been anyone from a door to door vacuum cleaner salesman to a serial killer. For a homicide detective, she was pretty loosey-goosey when it came to security. Of course, she did pack a big scary gun.

I walked through the tidy, southwest themed house and let myself into the back yard from the kitchen door. Peso, their enormous King German Shepherd, ran at full steam across the length of the yard to greet me. Thank goodness he was a lover, not a killer. I planted my feet and braced myself. There was no escaping this dog. A speeding freight train would be easier to slow down. He skidded to a stop and put his baseball mitt-sized front paws on my shoulders. He grinned and swiped his big tongue across my face with a slobbery doggie kiss. He got back on all fours and stuck his long, wet snoot in the back pocket of my jeans and fished out the milk bone I'd hidden.

AJ was decked out in LAPD bike shorts and a T-shirt. A *please do kiss the chef* apron and matching toque completed her cooking ensemble. She fiddled with one of the gas barbeque grids. "Thanks to you, now he picks everyone's pocket." She gave Peso a love scratch behind his ears. "Great career boost for a cop whose dog has a reputation as a pickpocket."

I took a deep bow. "I live to serve."

AJ Yakamura is a rail-thin, flat-chested, mouthy Asian woman with a dry sense of humor. I would never have paired her with mild-mannered Buster in a million years. She speaks fluent Spanish and Japanese in addition to English, is six inches taller and eight years younger than Buster, and takes crap from no one. She's whip-smart, dedicated, loyal to a fault, and loves Buster fiercely. Once a chain-smoking fiend who kicked the habit, a wad of bubble gum has replaced cigarettes.

I pecked AJ on the cheek and put my contribution of Chardonnay into the cooler. "Where's Buster?"

AJ used her hip to gently shove nosy Peso out of the way as she expertly buttered, salted, and wrapped three ears of corn in tin foil. "He called an hour ago. He was finishing with the Bikini Shop in Encino. He should be here any minute."

I muttered, "Not a chance. Even if he got there as the store opened, with phone interruptions, customer sales, and the salesgirls trying on all the samples, Buster could be there till midnight. Home soon for dinner? Ha. You can forget it. Breakfast was more likely. Steak and eggs, anyone?"

AJ popped a bubble the size of a newborn's head and pointed south toward LAX. "You got a plane to catch?"

My mouth watered at the pungent smell of the Asian-type seasoned marinade the three juicy steaks were soaking in. "I missed lunch today so I'm starving." I jabbed the barbeque fork at the steaks. "I want comfort food. I've had a tough day."

AJ snorted. "Good grief, don't tell me you found a second stiff. You're gonna get a reputation as the grim reaper of the mart."

I made a sour face. "Funny. Like passing a kidney stone. Not."

I uncorked the Chardonnay and poured each of us a glass. "I spent an extremely frustrating morning with Detective Miguel Martinez." I took a restorative glug and handed AJ her glass of wine. "You know him, right? What gives with this guy?"

"Yeah, I do. We were in the same class at the academy, but we've never worked together. His rep is he's tough as nails and a great cop. His case clearance rate is stellar." AJ put the ears of corn on the grill and sipped her wine. "You have a beef with Martinez?"

I waited for a half-dozen beats to choose my words. AJ and I were friends, but still, cops stick together. If I wanted her help with Martinez, I had to tiptoe around my opinion of the guy. "My friend Queenie and I had some vital information to give Martinez. This morning, we spent an extremely frustrating hour with him."

AJ took another sip of wine. "What information?"

"Some rather compelling evidence."

"What compelling evidence?"

"Proof someone else killed Bunny Frank."

She cocked an eyebrow. "And how did you manage to get this so-called compelling evidence?"

Oh yeah, like I'm gonna tell you. I repeated what I told Martinez.

Despite herself, AJ laughed out loud. “So, what did Martinez do?”

I rolled my eyes. “Took a couple of notes and asked a few questions.”

She gave me a look. “And you were expecting more?”

I pressed my lips into a tight line. “Yeah, more than a patronizing pat on the head.”

She laughed. “Come on; based on your say so, what, you were expecting him to release your friend from jail?”

Duh. “No, but when he promised to check it out, he warned it wouldn’t go anywhere because he already had Bunny’s killer behind bars.”

“Holly,” AJ lectured. “I realize Ms. Wilson is your friend and it doesn’t seem possible, but if they’re pushed far enough, even good people are capable of doing terrible things.” AJ sighed. “You’d be amazed at the number of upstanding citizens I’ve arrested.” She made quote marks in the air. “Perfectly lovely guy, the shocked neighbors all swore. It happens all the time.”

She was right, but this was Sonia Wilson, for crying out loud. “He’s either narrow-minded or taking the easy way out.”

AJ tsked. “He’s got nothing against Ms. Wilson personally. Martinez must have a lot of evidence, even if he didn’t share it with you.”

“I don’t care what he has. He’s wrong.”

“His rep is he’s a by the book cop. If he said he’d check out what you gave him, he will.”

I gave her a sideways glance. “Aren’t you curious what the information was?”

AJ held out her palms. “Honestly, no. The less I know, the better off we all are. If I was aware your evidence was obtained illegally, I’d be obligated to pass the information on. And if you got it illegally, the information is useless, the fruit of the poisoned tree. Secondly, it’s not my case, so unless he wanted my opinion, I’m in no position to tell him the way to run his investigation. It isn’t done.”

This was not going the way I’d planned. “He was waiting for the DNA and fingerprint tests to come back later today. He’s confident of getting an indictment.” Tears glistened the corners of my eyes. “We wanted to see Sonia.”

“And he told you no. The only visitors prisoners are permitted to have are their attorneys.”

I swiped at the tears wetting my cheeks. “You’re right. He told us to get there early for a seat in the gallery at the trial.” Anger burned like a fire in the pit of my stomach. “His parting shot was not to interfere with his investigation again or we’d be in the cell next to her.”

AJ had her cop face on. “It’s good advice. You ought to take it.” She pointed the barbeque fork at me. “Stay out of this. I’d hate for you to get tangled in a mess you might not be able to get out of.”

Like I had a choice.

A moment later, Buster walked into the backyard. A mouthwateringly delicious aroma filled the air as the steaks sizzled when they hit the grill, but I’d lost my appetite.

****

I faked my way through the motions of polite conversation, but I wasn’t into it. I ate a few bites not to be rude but mainly pushed the food around my plate. When AJ was busy talking, I snuck the steak under the table to my new bestie Peso. I was relieved we'd skipped dessert and called it an early night. I was angry and frustrated and frightened. We'd given Martinez so much evidence, and yet Sonia still sat in jail.

I got back to my houseboat and changed into my jammies. I wasn't in the mood for more conversation, so I turned off my cell phone. I clicked on the TV but nothing was appealing. I had enough drama in my life without Law and Order, and the comedies weren't funny. I needed a laugh, so I got into bed with a Joan Hess book. But I couldn't concentrate with the vision of Sonia behind bars in my head. I gave up after reading the same chapter three times. I tried to sleep, but the twist in my gut kept me awake. I tossed all night and finally threw in the towel at five. I hit the road before the crack of dawn, and the I-10 traffic snaking slowly east did nothing to improve my mood.

****

A Jolt of Java was packed and a challenge to get through the crowd. I took the tray of our preordered brews the barista had put to the side. Three idiots were too busy arguing over the date of the next market week to notice they were blocking the main aisle. To avoid wearing our drinks on my shirt, I went completely out of my way. I backed through the crowd and took a circuitous route like going to Newark by way of Nairobi to get to our table. I almost dropped the tray at the sound of Sonia Wilson's distinctively tinkly voice. "It took you long enough. Come on already and gimme my cuppa. The swill they passed off as coffee was pretty lousy at the hotel I was staying at."

I whirled around and stared at Sonia like she was an outer space alien. I put the tray on the table and cautiously touched her arm. I hadn't hallucinated it. She was really sitting there. She hugged me as fiercely as if we'd been separated by an ocean for several years.

I squawked, "When did you get out?"

"Last night at nine. Ms. Markowitz was there three hours earlier, but the paperwork took quite a while."

I asked, "What rabbit did Ms. Markowitz pull out of her briefcase?"

Sonia said, "I hadn't done anything wrong, so she had me volunteer a DNA swab along with the fingerprints they took. The DNA sample and fingerprints from the crime scene didn't match mine." Sonia's wide grin split her face in half. "Martinez tried to shuck and jive Ms. Markowitz into believing he still had enough circumstantial evidence to charge me. Boy, did she jump into action. She didn't take any crap from the guy." Sonia hooted. "She climbed on a chair and got right into his face. First, she quoted OJ's lawyer; if the glove doesn't fit, you must acquit. When Martinez didn't hop right to it, she warned if he didn't release her client in the next two minutes, by the time she was done with him, he'd be lucky if he got demoted to a meter maid in East LA."

A wave of relief washed over me until anger took its place. "So, you were out last night and gee whiz, ya didn't bother to call?"

Joan clucked her tongue. "She did."

Queenie tapped the front of her phone. "Check your voicemail once in a while."

Joan pursed her lips. "After her kids and parents, you were the first one she called."

The yentas bobbed in unison as Queenie pointed to each of them. “She called you, I called you. We all called you.” Queenie pushed the on- button of her mobile and waved the device in the air. “Here’s a news flash. These things work a lot better when they are turned on.”

Chapter Twenty-Three

I'd no sooner settled into my desk chair when Detective Martinez walked into the showroom. I gave him five attaboys for moxie. Facing me on my turf took some guts. I made no apology for the snark in my voice. "Detective, do you care for some coffee to go with your huge slice of humble pie?"

He grinned but had the grace to be abashed. "I guess I deserve that."

Gee, Columbo, nothing gets past you.

I studied Martinez through curious eyes. "Detective, I've already given you everything I had, and you weren't interested. Why are you here?"

Martinez held out his hands in supplication. "I'm back to square one, but now I'm between a rock and hard place."

I resisted the urge to say, "And whose fault is it?" Instead, I asked, "Meaning what?"

"After Ms. Wilson's DNA and fingerprints didn't match, we ran the crime scene evidence through the system and didn't get a single hit." Martinez used his pen cap to scratch the five o'clock shadow already darkening his chin. "So, now I've got some shaky circumstantial evidence to two men, and the science tells me to ignore it and find the woman who did the deed."

I held out my hands. "I appreciate your situation, but what is it you want from me?"

Martinez sighed. "Point me in the right direction."

I made a sour face. "I already did. I can't help it if the science doesn't match it. The science is wrong. You wanna nail Bunny's killer? Investigate Ronnie and Louis. They had the most to lose."

Martinez puckered his lips. "I walked by their showroom on my way over here and it's dark. Any idea where they are?"

I snarked, "Give me a sec and let me consult their calendars." I made a showing of opening a couple of drawers. "Sorry, I can't help you. They don't check their schedules in with me." I stared at the cop. "Detective, I still don't get what you want from me."

"Names."

This conversation had become annoyingly tedious. I had work to do. "Of who?"

Martinez impatiently tapped a drumbeat with his pen. His tone was peevish. "Obviously, women who had a problem with Ms. Frank."

I opened the top drawer of my desk and handed him the mart directory. "You'll find plenty of worthy candidates here. Knock yourself out."

Martinez handed me back the mart directory and glared. "You found Ms. Frank with a swimsuit stuffed in her mouth. Which women in your industry had problems with Ms. Frank?"

"Bunny Frank had problems of one kind or another with everyone, both men and women, in the swimwear industry." I waved the mart directory at the door. "All the swimwear vendors are on this floor. My suggestion is you go door to door."

Martinez snapped, "Ms. Schlivnik, if Ms. Frank deserves justice, get past our differences, and help me."

"Detective, I'm uncomfortable fingering a bunch of women whose only crime was not getting along with Bunny Frank." Nana's disapproving scowl floated across my mind. I sighed. "If you haven't already, talk to Margaret Adams. She's Bunny's office manager. If anyone knows where all the bodies in Bunny's graveyard are buried, it's Margaret. Go back to your notes on the day of the murder. I gave you five names. Start with them."

****

Two security guards with squawking walk-talkies and drawn batons flew past me like their hair was on fire. A huge crowd had gathered in front of the Clothing Concepts showroom blocking my view, so until the security team disbursed them, I had no idea what caused all the commotion.

The aisle cleared, and I found Hope standing in front of our door. I followed her eyes across the hall. A bloodied Ronnie and Louis each sat tied to a chair with their hands bound behind their backs with a security guard standing over them.

I jerked my chin to the CC showroom. "What's the story?"

Hope grinned. "Too bad you missed all the fireworks. I was on the phone with Buster taking a re-order, and there was a loud crash and a lot of yelling. I told Buster I had to call him back and ran out to see what was going on. When I got there, Ronnie and Louis were beating the crap out of one another. I was going to call security, but Joan already did."

Joan, Queenie, and Sonia moseyed over to add their fifty cents worth to the conversation.

Joan put her hands over her ears. "The crash was so loud it sounded like a ceiling had collapsed."

Sonia said, "Tables and chairs were tossed around like in a hurricane. The sample racks were ripped out of the walls, and swimsuits were scattered all over the room."

Queenie said, "Good thing security got here as fast as they did, or the two idiots would have killed one another."

Sonia asked, "What were they fighting over?"

I said, "Bet they met with Detective Martinez again."

Joan nodded her agreement. "Sounds right. When I got there, they were screaming at the top of their lungs, trying to pin Bunny's murder on the other guy."

Sonia held her wristwatch out. "Sorry to spoil the party, but I've got some appointment rescheduling to do." She grinned. "Come get me if the two golden gloves go for a second round." Sonia went back to her showroom and narrowly missed bumping into Angela Wellborn.

Angela stammered. "S-Sonia? What are you doing here? Weren't you arrested?"

"I was released the night before last."

Angela clapped Sonia on the shoulder. "Great news. I never believed you did it. I'm so glad you were cleared. How did you manage it?"

"Their evidence didn't hold up." Sonia pointed at me. "And Holly got me a fantastic lawyer."

Angela smiled warmly. "Wonderful. I'm glad it all worked out. I hear your line has a couple of hot styles. Call me so we can set something up."

Sonia promised she would and went into her showroom.

Angela pushed the Clothing Concepts door open, but she was stopped by the security guard. Her tone was demanding. “What’s going on here?” The guard didn’t answer, so Angela tried to go around him, but he blocked her way. “Miss, the showroom is closed. You can’t come in here.”

Angela motioned to Louis and growled like a mama bear. “Get outta my way! Can’t you tell he’s hurt?”

The security guard ignored her questions and forced her out the door.

Angela stomped over to us. “The guard wouldn’t tell me a thing. What’s going on?”

Joan said, “Frazier and Ali were beating the tar out of one another till the mart security broke up the fight.”

One look at the disaster across the hall and Angela gasped, “It looks like a bomb hit the place. What were they fighting over?”

I said, “In between punches, they were accusing one another of being Bunny Frank’s killer.”

Angela gave me an odd look. “Why?”

I filled in the blanks. “After Sonia was cleared, the detective investigating Bunny’s murder has been interviewing suspects. They probably had another interview with him.”

Angela’s eyes lit with recognition. “The cop? What’s his name again? Mar-something or other, right?” Angela squeezed her eyes closed.

I prompted, “Martinez?”

Angela nodded. “Yeah, he’s the guy.” She hiccupped a nervous laugh. “How could I forget his name? He was in my office for almost two hours questioning me yesterday. Lucky for me, I was with Ernie in nonstop meetings all day on the day of the murder. If the boss hadn't backed my story, I can't imagine what would have happened? The cop challenged all my answers." Angela pressed her lips together. "The night of the murder I was at a nursery buying perennials. I had to dig out the receipts before he believed me."

I pointed to Louis and Ronnie. "For my money, one of them did it. Ronnie had one heck of a motive." I smiled to lessen the blow. "You don't want to hear it, but Louis had the most to lose."

Angela's kinky hair swung from side to side when she shook her head no. "No way. Ronnie is an arrogant bully, but he's all foam and no beer. And Louis?" Angela's eyes shone. "My man? He couldn't do it." Angela fluttered her fingers at the Clothing Concepts showroom. "I'll get the story later from Louis." She tsked. "Ronnie's a trouble-maker. No doubt, he instigated whatever this was."

Angela and a livid Martin Decker danced around one another as she went to the elevator bank and he marched into his showroom.

I jerked my chin at the two restrained men. "What's gonna happen to those two now?"

Joan quirked a smile. "If Martin doesn't fire them, he might kill them himself."

A half-hour later, Louis and Ronnie left the destroyed showroom with Martin and the security guard. By the end of the day, the front windows of the showroom had been boarded with sheets of plywood. The lights were on and the sounds of power drills and hammers banging echoed through the aisle. When all the drilling and hammering stopped, would Louis and Ronnie be back to reopen their showroom?

Two swimwear industry executives beat the crap out of one another while arguing over which one of them murdered Bunny Frank.

Cripes, this was one heck of a day.

Chapter Twenty-Four

Queenie and I got the last table in the back of the mart deli conveniently located ladies' room adjacent. We settled into our seats at a tiny two-top meant for contortionist midgets and gave our regular server Laura our order.

Queenie slurped iced tea and frowned. "Whaddya make of Louis and Ronnie using one another as punching bags?"

"My guess is Bunny's murder was a collaborative effort and it went off the rails. And now they're trying to save their own asses by fingering each other."

Queenie squeezed a lemon wedge into her tea glass. "Did Martin fire them?"

I blew out my cheeks. "He should, but I bet he didn't."

Queenie crossed her eyes. "Why not? After all the shenanigans they've pulled, if I were Martin, those two clowns would be out on the curb with the trash by now."

"They may not last past this season, but for now, a statement of a united front to the market is the smartest thing Martin can do to minimize the mess those two morons made."

Queenie wrinkled her brow. "Is Detective Martinez gonna arrest one of them?"

I bit my lip. "Nah, at least not now. Martinez can't wrap his arms around the concept the killer could be a he instead of a she. Unless one of them confesses or a smoking gun magically appears, Martinez isn't gonna arrest either one of them."

Queenie said, "On my way to meet you, I walked past Clothing Concepts. The construction crew must have worked all night. It's like the fight never happened. No sign Ali and Frasier had torn the place apart." Queenie wiggled her brows. "Maybe now someone can locate the smoking gun…"

****

Queenie wrapped her fingers around the door handle. "Shall we?"

I took a step closer. "No time like the present."

Queenie pushed the glass door and surprisingly, it opened. She waved me through. "Age before beauty."

I called, "Hello? Anybody home?"

Nothing.

Queenie asked, "If nobody's here why's the door open?"

Good question.

I eyed the vacant reception desk. "Where's the mousy-faced receptionist?"

Queenie motioned to the hallway. "Gone. After the first punch was thrown, she duck-walked around Louis and Ronnie and ran out the door. She called human resources from home to quit, told them to mail her paycheck, and swore she'd never step foot in the showroom as long as those two maniacs were there."

I groused, "If the two maniacs are in the back, they're deaf as doornails. Don't they hear us yelling?"

Queenie sniffed, "Or, more likely, the two jerks are ignoring us." She motioned to the entrance. "They should put a bell or a buzzer or something on the door."

Queenie giggled. "Can you imagine Sue Ellen coming in and the reception desk is vacant? She yells hello and nobody drops what they're doing and jumps out to greet her? Whaddya think she'd do to those two clowns?"

The thought made me shudder. "Let's check if either of the golden gloves is present."

"If they are, why are we here?"

I arched my brows. "Concerned neighbors checking in on them?"

Queenie made the gag sign. "And if not, what are we looking for now?"

"Dunno. Like the last time. We'll know it when we see it."

"It better jump out pretty fast and say howdy." Queenie pointed to the abandoned reception desk. "With nobody manning the front, they won't be gone too long."

I pivoted towards the offices. "Time's a-wasting."

We stood in the main hallway leading to the offices and yelled 'hello' a half dozen times. No replies. We went to the far corner and worked our way back. Curious. The place was lit like a Broadway theater marquee on opening night, but the cast was nowhere to be found.

"Same as last time?"

I lifted a shoulder. "If it's not broke, don't fix it."

Queenie followed me into Ronnie's office, and we stopped dead in our tracks. The loveseat was completely covered with pants, jeans, and shirts. Ronnie's skivvies were stacked on the coffee table along with a black leather travel kit. Three large leather suitcases and two garment bags sat side by side next to the sofa. Ronnie's suits and sports jackets were hung on the sample rack in front of the swimsuits.

"I guess Mrs. Schwartzman had enough of her husband's shenanigans and threw him out of the house."

Queenie patted the table with the pile of Ronnie's silk skivvies. "No kidding. He's moved in for the duration."

"Weird he's camping out in his office and not on his boat. Why air his dirty laundry to the industry?"

Queenie opened the middle drawer of his files and said, "I'd be surprised if it ever crossed his mind. He's way too arrogant to care. The only opinion important to him is his own."

I sat at Ronnie's desk. "He can't be too far so ten minutes max this time."

Before Queenie could reply, Ronnie's Schwartzman's battered body filled the doorframe. His evil sneer stole my breath away. "Nah, it's gonna be a lot less this time."

The best way to describe his appearance? Like he'd been hit by a bus. An uncontrollable tic in his is left eye winked open and shut like a broken traffic signal. His right eye was swollen three-quarters closed and ringed by an ugly yellow-tinged purple and black shiner. His splinted cauliflower nose leaned to the left. His left arm was in a sling, and two bandaged fingers on his right hand were taped together.

Queenie tried to discreetly close the middle file drawer with her tush, but the drawer stuck and squeaked a loud complaint. With me sitting behind his desk holding one of his folders, the chances of Ronnie believing we were there out of concern for him were slimsky to nonesky. With Plan A out the window and no other options, I punted to smart-mouthing our way out of this mess. I waved at his wardrobe spread out across the furniture. “Busman’s holiday or did the wife finally throw your sorry ass out of the fancy mansion?”

Ronnie made a feeble attempt to lunge at me, but with his left arm in a sling, he had trouble pulling his bulky body through the doorframe. His two missing front teeth garbled his speech. “You’ve got some mout on you, conthidering I caught you wed-handed. I should call thecurity and have you awested for bweaking and entewing.”

Queenie sneered. “Nice try, bucko. We did no such thing. Your door was open.”

I smirked. “So, where’s Louis? You finally get around to knocking him off too?”

Ronnie’s nostrils flared like a galloping stallion. He took more time with his words. “I knew it. You two were the ones who pointed the cop at me.”

Yikes. Had Martinez given us up?

I scoffed. “Why would you say something so ridiculous?”

“You two are jealous of me.”

Were there no limits to his self-absorbed arrogance?

With some effort, Ronnie lifted his right arm and waved it around the room. “With me out of the way, you two can tag team Martin and take over the empire I built from nothing.” He stabbed a bandaged index finger into his chest. “Over my dead body.” Ronnie bared his teeth like a rabid coyote. “I catch you two anywhere near this office again, they won’t find enough left of you to identify.”

A wildly beating pulse roared in my ears, and my knees knocked together like a couple of bowling pins. My dad taught his children to never show fear, always confront it. I spread my arms open wide. David calling out Goliath on the eleventh floor of the mart. “Enjoy your empire while you still can, because it won’t be long before it’s all gone. You’re going to lose everything.” Bravado mixed with conviction masked the tentacles of fear gripping my heart. “We don’t have to push you over the cliff. You’re going to fall all on your own.”

Little did I realize my words of warning would prove to be so prophetic.

Chapter Twenty-Five

It had rained all day when I got to the mart parking structure and discovered the flat tire. This is LA. It doesn't rain much here, so no one knows how to drive in it. The Santa Monica freeway probably resembled a demolition derby track by now. But when it rains, it rains cats and dogs day and night. We're not talking a leaky faucet. Think grab all the animals and build the Ark kind of rain.

If I called the auto club and luck broke my way, maybe they'd have a tow truck to the mart by next Tuesday. For giggles and squeaks, I called anyway on the off chance I underestimated their inclement weather preparedness. As if. I got a recording thanking me for my many years as a loyal customer and asking to please accept their sincere apologies for any inconvenience they were causing, but they were too busy to help me with my problem for the foreseeable future. To add insult to injury, the recording disconnected me. Twice.

Fortunately, my dad insisted his kids learn to change a tire. I opened the trunk, hauled the spare out, along with the jack and a heavy lug wrench. Before I positioned the jack under the jack point, I rolled my sleeves and cringed. I had worn an expensive lavender silk blouse and a new pair of gray gabardine pants for the first time. Spiffy ensemble, but not the best outfit to play grease monkey.

Was there a knight in shining armor? I checked around the garage. I might be an independent woman, but my mother didn't raise stupid children. I waited for ten minutes, but no hero appeared. No doubt he was at happy hour getting sloshed with all the other heroes waiting out the storm. I couldn't sit around all night waiting for help to arrive. I gritted my teeth and reasoned the guy who ran the dry cleaners had kids I'd be helping to put through college.

I got the car jacked, the lug nuts off, and switched out the flat with the spare without ruining my trousers. I ran my fingers over the flat. There is always a lot of construction around the mart. Maybe I ran over a nail? Sure enough, there was a big fat one embedded deep in the tread. I shoved the flat and the changing kit in the trunk and drove to the gas station. Johnny, the owner, swapped my flat for another spare, and I headed to the marina and a gigantic glass of Chardonnay.

The next evening, the mustang listed to the left so badly, the flat was visible from the elevator bank. The auto club guy changed the flat and put on the tire Johnny patched the day before. The first one, okay an inconvenience, especially with the rain, but no biggie; everyone gets a flat tire. But two days in a row? Cripes, give me a break.

The next day had been a challenge. Nothing had gone right, and I was anxious to get home. The last thing I needed was another problem, but when I got to the mustang, another flat tire. Figure the odds. Better go to Vegas and bet the farm. My luck, I got the same auto club guy from the previous evening. When he suggested I ditch the car and consider public transportation, I gave the smartass the mental middle finger salute. Another comedian.

I drove back to the station and left the mustang with Johnny. Three flats in three days? Get real. I had enough. I wanted answers. Queenie met me at the station, shuttled me home, and the next morning gave me a lift to the mart. Before I even sat at my desk, the phone was ringing. Johnny was on the line. All four tires were damaged and had to be replaced. Cripes. The week had become a doozy.

I put my purse in the bottom drawer and noticed a plain white envelope with my name typed on the front sitting on my blotter. I waved it at Hope. "Who left this?"

She shook her head. "No idea. It was on the floor when I opened the showroom this morning."

I slit the envelope and unfolded a single sheet of paper. My blood ran cold when I read the first line.

"Holy crap," I choked. "Hope, come over here."

Hope's voice shook with alarm. "What's the matter? You're white as a ghost." She read the note and took a step back as though fending off a blow. "Oh my God."

Someone had cut out the letters from magazines so the note spelled a threat and a deadly warning:

DoN'T STicK yOuR NosE WherE It DOesN'T BeLOng

Or yOU wIlL ENd Up ThE SamE wAy aS bUnNy fRANk

mIND yOUr OwN BUsinEsS YoU HavE BEeN wARnEd

Queenie walked into our showroom holding the same note. We left the Rampart division station mad as wet hens. Detective Martinez's reaction to the threatening notes? Chastise us for interfering again with his case.

After enduring a blistering lecture from AJ on the merits of minding my own business and possibly staying alive, I spent a restless night pacing my houseboat questioning what the heck I was doing.

****

The mustang was still with Johnny, so the next morning, Queenie and I carpooled to the mart. Queenie sported the same dark circles under her eyes like mine. Frustration and fear had kept us both awake the night before.

I slid into my seat at the yenta table hoping for answers, and if not, sympathetic ears. After I described my troubling conversation with AJ, Queenie sighed. "I dunno Hol, your friend is right. Maybe we should listen to her and let this go?" Queenie pointed her coffee cup at Sonia. "We got into it to help Sonia. She doesn't need our help anymore. Why don't we throw in the towel and let Detective Martinez do his job?"

The rational side of me agreed. After all, hadn't I spent the night before saying the same thing? Yet the stubborn part of me wasn't prepared to let go. So far, the detective's batting average was the same dismal one as ours. Someone had viciously murdered a prominent industry big wig right under our noses. Maybe Bunny Frank was only the first victim. What if she wasn't the last? Who could be next? Till Bunny's killer was captured, none of us were safe.

I jutted my chin. "I don't see how we can."

Chapter Twenty-Six

My mind was still in a tizzy when Queenie dropped me off at Johnny's. I got out my checkbook, but Johnny wanted me to see the damaged tires first. I followed him into the service bay. My four tires were on a rack. Johnny bounced the first one to the ground. "I don't want to scare you, but these tires have been tampered with."

My heart leaped into my throat. I parroted, "Tampered with?" I squinted, but if there was a problem, I didn't see it. The tire was like all the others on the rack, perfectly normal. Wasn't it?

Johnny laid the tire on its side and squatted next to it. He ran a grease-stained thumb around the edge. "The tread is barely worn. If there wasn't a shard or a nail, air pressure is right, and nothing wrong with the valve, no reason for a tire to go flat."

I gave it the once-over and still didn't see anything. "Sorry, I don't see anything wrong with it."

He angled the tire. "It's not visible with the naked eye. We filled the tires with air, and they went flat again. We ran them through the tester, and we couldn't find a nail or any glass. We filled one with air again, and once we submerged it in water, we found the source." Johnny guided my finger to a spot on the inner part of the tread with some tape over it. "These tires were punctured with an ice pick. The leak was slow so you wouldn't notice it. This could have been a lot worse. You could have had a blowout at a high speed on the freeway."

I leaned over the tire. What was I missing? "How can you be so sure it was an icepick?"

"By the shape and width of the puncture and the way the air came out of the submerged tire." Johnny's expression was grave. "Somebody wanted to hurt you badly."

Martinez arrived and examined the tire and called in the lab.

I pointed to the tire. "Detective, either Ronnie Schwartzman or Louis Chennault could have done this. They know Queenie and I burgled their offices and we pointed you in their direction. This is payback. There's a full bar in their office. Betcha find an icepick."

Martinez said, "No question, you've got somebody's attention. It is still unclear as to who." He narrowed his eyes. "This isn't payback, Ms. Schlivnik; it's a warning and one you should heed. Stay out of this and let me do my job before you're the next victim."

"I'm getting close to something, but to what, I can't say yet." I grinned. "Give me some time, and I'll piss them off enough to find out."

Martinez pursed his lips. "This is no joking matter. You're in their crosshairs, and now you've painted a target on your back. You've been lucky so far in this game of cat and mouse, but the odds aren't with you. Remember. Players sometimes get lucky and win a few hands, but sooner or later, you'll overplay yours and lose. Eventually, the house always wins."

My head was reeling. First, a threatening letter, and now someone had messed with my car. Either Ronnie or Louis had to be responsible. We all park in the same parking structure. My cotton-candy pink convertible wasn't hard to pick out. How difficult would it be for them to tamper with my tires? Not hard at all. We must be getting close to proving they murdered Bunny. Would Detective Martinez agree before one of them damaged more than my car?

****

I had my hand on our showroom door handle when Detective Martinez and two LAPD uniforms brushed past me. Ten minutes later, Louis Chennault was sandwiched between the two uniforms with his wrists shackled behind his back. An icepick encased in a plastic evidence bag was in the detective's hand.

Queenie marched into our showroom right after the law enforcement entourage got into the elevator. "We just found out."

I did a doubletake. Stop the presses. The megaphone of the mart was not the first to report the big news? Telephone, telegraph, tell Queenie. CNN had nothing on Queenie Levine.

The curiosity was killing me. "Where were you guys? You're directly across from them. How could you possibly miss it?"

Joan joined the cabal. "We were in the back office on the phones. The commotion in the hallway got us out to see what all the fuss was. A crowd had gathered in front of Clothing Concepts. Michael Rothman told us Louis had been arrested." Joan funneled her lips. "How could we miss all the excitement?"

Queenie pinched in her face. "I guess Martinez pulled his head out of his ass and checked on the stuff we gave him."

I said, “He found an icepick in the Clothing Concepts office as I told him he would. Maybe he finally gets we’re not a couple of chuckleheads playing around. But Ronnie should have been arrested too.”

Queenie shook her head. “I dunno. Martinez wasn’t too impressed with the ledger.”

I laughed. “He also said the only thing Bunny’s letter proved is she was a couple of tacos short of a combination.”

Queenie mused, “But what if she wasn’t? Louis’ career was over if she made good on her threat. Maybe he couldn’t take a chance and shut her up for good.”

Joan tapped her fingertip on her lips. “I’ve got a couple of friends at the Clothing Concepts factory. Lemme sniff around. There might be somebody willing to talk.”

Angela Wellborn walked in white as a ghost. “I went into Gotham to meet Louis. We had a lunch date.” Angela’s fist flew to her lips as she let out a sob. “Ronnie said Louis has been arrested.” Her eyes filled as she searched our group. “There must be some mistake.”

Angela stiffened when I put an arm around her shoulder. “Angela, I’m sorry, but it’s true. Detective Martinez and two uniform patrolmen escorted Louis out of the showroom in handcuffs.” I couldn’t soften the blow. “Angela, remember the other day Louis and Ronnie had the big fight? I said Ronnie had a motive to kill Bunny but Louis had the most to lose?” She nodded yes, so I continued. “Before the fight took place, I had a flat tire for three nights in a row. I’m telling you this because my tires had been tampered with. Someone took an icepick and punctured the tires.”

She grimaced. “Geez, how awful. But what does it have to do with Louis getting arrested?”

I said, “I can’t go into the details, but I’d given the detective some information regarding Louis and Ronnie. They had their fistfight after Detective Martinez interviewed them a second time. Louis must have figured out I gave the detective the information and tampered with my tires to send me a message.”

Angela huffed, “You’re out of your mind.”

“No, I’m not. When Louis was arrested, Martinez was holding an icepick in an evidence bag. It will likely match the punctures in my tires.”

Angela sniffed. “And what if it does? Ronnie could just as easily tamper with your tires.”

“You’re right. But he didn’t.”

She glowered, “How do you know?”

I held out my hands in supplication. “You’re right, I don’t, but Martinez must. Louis is the one he arrested, not Ronnie.”

Angela wriggled out of my grasp and glared. “You’re wrong. Louis is innocent. Wait and see.”

Chapter Twenty-Seven

I had a late afternoon appointment with Sue Ellen Magee. Samples were hung on the grid; the Bainbridge file folder was open, and two copies of the proposal were printed. I was all set. Where the heck was Sue Ellen? I checked the time twice to be sure I read it right. Alert the media. Sue Ellen Magee was forty-five minutes late. This is one buyer who was never late and expected you to be prompt, as no excuse was acceptable. Her time was valuable, but not yours. Unless you were lying dead in a ditch, you'd better not dare keep this buyer waiting.

She finally dragged herself in an hour late muttering her apologies. I debated whether to ask her to repeat it. Considering she's never wrong, shocking she was capable of uttering the words. Had the always in control Sue Ellen Magee been run over by a freight train? Fatigue lines cratered her cheeks, dark circles smudged her eyelids, and she sputtered her words like a leaky faucet as she slumped in the chair. Something had cut the Iron Maiden down several notches. What?

With all the grief she'd given me, the stab of pity took me by surprise. "It's getting late. Would you like a little pick me up?"

"Like what?"

Was she expecting a menu? "How's a Coke sound?"

She honked out a reply like a cross between a sob and a snort. "Coke? Got anything stronger?"

Was this the mart or Cheers?

I offered an apology even though I wasn't the least bit sorry. "Gee, I'm sorry, all we've got is bottled water, Coke, and Dr. Browns."

As though she was doing me a great favor, she grunted, "Oh, all right. If those are the only choices, a Diet Coke if you've got it. In a cup, not in the can."

Apparently, please and thank you were not part of her vocabulary. The demand in her tone was annoying, but to be honest, I was relieved. This nasty version wasn't pleasant, but at least this is the person I expected. I served her the soda in a cup, not in the can. "You ok? You seem a bit off your feed."

She snapped, "Put a cork in it, will ya? I've had a helluva day."

Atta girl. Way more like it. Welcome back. The real Sue Ellen Magee. The one we all love to hate. We stared at each other for a few awkward minutes while I waited for her to elaborate. She swallowed a glug of soda and grimaced. "An LAPD homicide detective came to my office this afternoon. He questioned me for almost two hours. It's the reason why I was late."

An unsettling thought flitted across my brain. Was I sitting across from Bunny's killer? My pulse beat a staccato rhythm in my throat. The closest things we had to a weapon were a pair of pinking shears and an attachment gun that shoots little plastic loops to fasten the hang tags onto the bikinis. Not exactly a lethal arsenal. Cripes. Wasn't it time for Ernesto to make his rounds? The old guy was no Rambo, but he had a Taser and a walkie talkie. I slid my eyes toward the aisle.

There was no one in the dark hallway. Sue Ellen and I were all alone. Not a soul on the floor, not a warm body anywhere in sight. I was on my own. Gulp.

Sue Ellen groused, "And the stuff the cop hit me with? Every problem I ever had with Bunny." There was a tone of surprise in her complaint. "He wasn't buying any of my explanations."

Imagine the nerve of the guy? I needed the business, so I restrained myself from gloating.

Sue Ellen squawked like a plucked hen. "How embarrassing. He questioned my boss on the rumor Bunny spread." Her voice shook. "And my promotion being in jeopardy." Stop the presses. Did I detect a touch of fear in Fearless Fosdick's tone? "He asked where I was when Bunny was murdered."

Sue Ellen opened the door, and I walked right in. "Sue Ellen, your problems with Bunny aren't exactly a state secret. If you don't mind me asking, where were you when Bunny was murdered?"

Sue Ellen's jaw dropped so far, it only missed hitting the table by inches. Oh, joy; I managed to piss off this powerful buyer even more. The way the meeting was going, cancel these orders would be the next thing out of her mouth. If I'd been sitting, I would have fallen out of my chair when she laughed. "The only reason I'm not in a jail cell is I had an airtight alibi. I was in San Diego the day Bunny was killed in a meeting with a dozen regional managers at our Fashion Valley store. After the meeting, I took the group out to dinner at Bully's Steakhouse in La Jolla. The next morning, I had a meeting with the display department and didn't get back to LA till late the next afternoon." A flash of anger darkened her eyes. "I had to produce copies of all my receipts, or I swear, he was gonna cuff me." Sue Ellen chugged the rest of her soda and handed me the empty cup. She focused her attention on the suits I'd hung on the grid. "I presume you got me everything I want." She smiled a devilish grin. "It's been a tough day. Be a darned shame if I had to take it out on you."

Between her badass attitude and unreasonable demands, Sue Ellen Magee was always a handful. Once she brought her personal problems into the showroom, this time she was utterly exhausting. I couldn't get to the marina fast enough. After a session like this one, I needed a pizza and a big glass of wine, intravenously, if possible. As I unlocked the car, I could practically taste the pepperoni.

I dropped the top on the mustang and settled into the seat. I twisted the key in the ignition, but the two-eighty-nine didn't roar to life. All I got were a series of metallic clicks and nothing. Fantfreakingtastic. Cripes. First flat tires, now a dead battery? At this rate, I'd have to put the auto club on speed dial.

Triple-A was apparently in no big hurry to answer my call. It took two hours for the tow truck to arrive. The service guy connected the jumper cables to my battery. I keyed the ignition, but the engine still didn't turn over. Weird. The battery was two months old, practically brand new. The auto club guy leaned under the hood and poked around. He took the cables off the battery. "Nothing's wrong with the battery. You've got a bigger problem." He motioned for me to look where he was pointing. "See the wire connecting to the ignition coil with nothing on the other end? Your distributor cap is missing. You're not going anywhere without it."

****

I dialed Queenie's number long past the polite time to call. She denied it, but I could tell I'd woken her. She didn't need an explanation, and I didn't offer one. Queenie pulled into Johnny's station five minutes after the tow truck lowered the mustang off the flatbed. I locked the car and left Johnny a note under a windshield wiper.

We got back to the marina and stopped at Tiny Maylor's on Lincoln. I'd missed dinner and was famished. I ordered a jumbo burger combo and coffee.

Queenie added a splash of cream to her coffee. "A dead battery wasn't the reason your car wouldn't start?"

I shook my head. "Nope. The battery was fine."

"So, why didn't the car start?"

"The distributor cap."

"What's wrong with it?"

I twisted my lips into a wry smile. "There's nothing wrong with it except it isn't in the engine."

"Did it get loose or something?"

I shook my head. "No, it couldn't from where it's located on the engine block."

She joked, "Did you misplace it? Try checking your purse."

A regular comedian.

She gave me the big eyes. "How do you lose a distributor cap?"

How indeed?

Should I level with her? Absolutely. I owed her the truth, even if it meant a midnight call to Detective Martinez and another lecture. If I used my brain, I'd have already called him, but no one ever confused me with Albert Einstein.

First punctured tires, now a missing distributor cap. What was next? Stripped brake lines? Cripes. This was now personal. I had to get to the bottom of this. "You're right. Nobody loses a distributor cap. Somebody purposely removed it. We must be getting close to cracking this case, and somebody's getting nervous. The question is who?"

Queenie dropped me off at the top of why bother with going to bed o'clock. I took a hot shower and changed my clothes. I brewed a pot of strong coffee and parked my tush at the galley table to figure this mess out. If the auto club guy was right, I'd pissed somebody off big time. Several worthy candidates made the hit parade.

Car buff Louis Chennault was the obvious choice, but he was currently a guest at the Graybar hotel. I crossed him off the list. Strike one.

Could Prima Donna Ronnie Schwartzman tell the difference between a distributor cap and a baseball cap? As if. Strike number two.

Not the sharpest knife in the drawer, could Michael Rothman spell distributor cap, much less know where to find it in the engine block? Strike three, and I was out.

Who else was there? I flipped through my mental Rolodex. Angela Wellborn. She was certainly familiar enough with a car engine to remove the distributor cap. But tampering with the mustang over a contested order cancellation? Good grief, get real.

****

I was on my second pot of coffee but no further along when the sun peeked through the aft porthole. I poured coffee into two commuter cups, shouldered my messenger bag, and headed for the gangplank. Queenie was already parked in front of my basin. Not exactly a morning person, this was probably Queenie Levine's first sunrise. She hungrily glugged the mug dry in two gulps. She grunted something resembling good morning, but I couldn't be sure.

Queenie dropped me off at Johnny's station, and Detective Martinez was in the service bay with his head under the mustang's hood. I gave Johnny the big eyes. Johnny gave them right back. "This was no accident. Somebody messed with the car twice in one week." Johnny smiled sheepishly and shrugged. "He's a cop. Who else are ya gonna call?"

Who indeed?

Chapter Twenty-Eight

I muscled my way through the crowd at the mart newsstand. The West Coast Apparel News headline above the fold screamed:

Major Shake-Up At CC: Copycat Chennault Out at Clothing Concepts

Sonia scanned the headline and cocked a brow. "Wait a minute. Wasn't Louis Chennault just arrested? So, now he's out? Out of what? Out of jail? Out of a job? Out of his mind? Out of luck?"

Joan laughed. "All of the above. He was released from jail and fired the same day."

Hope asked, "Do you know what happened?"

Joan surveyed the table. "The mystery woman was Louis' alibi, but he still refused to reveal her identity. Martinez could hold Louis for seventy-two hours without charging him. The scuttlebutt is the detective put Louis in a cell and threatened to throw away the key if Louis didn't cough up the woman's name."

Sonia blinked with confusion. "Where was Louis' lawyer during all this? Ms. Markowitz was with me the entire time Martinez questioned me. No way she'd have let Martinez intimidate me into a trap."

Joan funneled her lips. "According to my CC contact, Louis waived his right to a lawyer. Claimed he was innocent and didn't need one."

Sonia's eyes bugged. "What a moron."

Joan said, "Louis spent the night and half the next day locked up before he cracked."

Queenie smirked. "Joanie, tell them who the mystery woman was."

Joan's grin was as wide as a Jack O'Lantern. "None other than Shannon Decker."

I squeaked, "As in Mrs. Martin Decker?"

Joan grinned. "One and the same. My friend Crystal said the now no doubt soon to be ex-Mrs. Decker and Louis met at the company Christmas party. It's come out they've had a nooner Tuesdays and Thursdays for half a year. Anyway, when Louis gave her up, Martinez had her brought in. At first, she denied the affair, but when the detective threatened her with perjury and obstruction, Shannon Decker folded like a cheap card table."

Sonia pointed to the newspaper headline. "But Louis got fired for impersonating a designer, not for boffing the boss's wife."

Joan folded the newspaper in sections and fluttered it like a fan. "Don't always believe what you read. Martin Decker's saving face. He's not gonna air their dirty laundry for all the industry to see. The design issue was a major factor of why Louis was let go, but the real reason he got canned was for boffing the boss's wife."

Hope asked, "Did Angela have any idea?"

Queenie shook her head. "If love is blind, Angela is Helen Keller."

Hope tsked. "Poor Angela. She's over the moon for the guy. This is gonna kill her."

Sonia smirked, "This is what happens when men think with the wrong head."

****

With Louis Chennault off the suspect list and no smoking gun pointing at Ronnie Schwartzman, I was out of ideas. No one knew Bunny and her legion of enemies like Margaret Adams. I called her for an opinion on which one of them might have knocked off her boss.

Margaret said, "I'll tell you the same thing I told Detective Martinez. Miss Frank was pushy and demanding. She did whatever it took to get what she wanted and didn't care what happened to anyone who got in her way. But for all her rotten traits, Miss Frank also did a lot of good for the apparel industry. Miss Frank's influence was instrumental for many fledgling companies like Clothing Concepts to becoming powerhouses and made a lot of people rich. But most of all, Miss Frank forced the industry to be the best it could be. Not only did she demand it, but she'd eat someone for breakfast if they weren't at the top of their game. If you want to find who killed Miss Frank, find the person who didn't measure up to her standards."

****

I called Ellen Thomas to tell her I was coming to her office to deliver a check for an outstanding invoice. I took the old-fashioned elevator with its grilled cage door to the fifth level of the art-deco BO-LAR building where the Acme Buying Office occupied the entire floor. I signed in, got a visitor's badge, and followed Ellen's assistant Tiffany into the executive suite. She rapped on Ellen's office door twice and opened it. The Acme Vice President was finishing a phone call and waved us in. I declined Tiffany's offer of something to drink, and she left, closing the door behind her.

Ellen put the phone back in its cradle. "I appreciate your coming over. But delivering the check personally? Such service." She barked out a laugh. "It's the height of the swimwear season. Is your business so slow you don't have better things to do with your time?" Ellen's smile didn't reach her cold gray eyes. "We've pretty much finished our business with your line, so why don't you tell me why you're really here?"

So much for a clever pretext. With no reason to quibble, I got right to it. "I'm investigating Bunny Frank's murder and I want to ask you some questions."

Ellen leaned forward like a vulture ready to pounce on its prey. "And why would I know anything?"

"It's common knowledge you had major issues with Bunny."

Ellen rolled her eyes. "Who didn't?"

No argument there. "The word on the street is Bunny was stealing your accounts left and right, and if you didn't put a stop to it, you could lose your job." My eyes bored into hers. "I was right there when you threatened Bunny at the ISAM party."

Ellen fluttered her fingers. "It meant nothing. I was trying to score a few points with an important client. As to my boss firing me?" Ellen slapped the desk and hooted, "Osborne Bradley threatens to fire me at least twice a day over something. I've been here a dozen years. His threats are a lot of hot air."

I looked her in the eye. "Ellen, are you and Osborne Bradley an item?"

Her head snapped back as though she'd been struck. "What kind of question is that?"

I shrugged. "A pretty straightforward one. So, are you, or aren't you?"

She sniffed, "It's none of your business, but no. Even if I was, what does it have to do with Bunny Frank?" Ellen laughed. "If this is where you're going, you can forget a love triangle gone bad. She wasn't his type." Ellen narrowed her eyes. "Why would you even ask such a question?"

"Hear tell a pretty interesting conversation between you and Osborne took place in the mart parking lot not long ago."

She scoffed, "I work for the man. We have lots of conversations."

"Not like this one."

Ellen gave me the big eyes. "Meaning?"

"Meaning you were overheard professing your undying love for him and telling him there is nothing in the world you wouldn't do to prove your love."

Ellen snarled like a rabid dog. "It's a filthy lie. Never happened. Whoever said it, they're lying through their teeth."

"Several people repeated it, and their story was the same." I held my hands out in supplication. "I don't give a fig for your relationship with him, except it goes to motive."

She blinked with confusion. "How?"

"Taking out Bunny killed a whole flock of birds with one stone. You knock off the competition, stop client defections, and prove to Osborne Bradley you would do anything for him." I dipped my head. "Or maybe he promised to take your relationship to the next level if you got rid of Bunny Frank." I lifted a shoulder. "It could have happened either way."

Ellen's eyes turned hard as granite. "The man couldn't tell you the color of my eyes if his life depended on it." Ellen's bitter laugh came out as a sob. "He pays a lot more attention to the potted plants."

Was she a helluva actress or had I hit a bullseye? "Where were you when Bunny was murdered?"

Ellen snapped, "I've already spoken with the police."

"Bet you didn't mention how close you are to the boss." I flashed her a killer smile. "Martinez might be pretty interested in your relationship with Osborne Bradley."

Ellen sniffed, "I don't have to answer any of your questions."

"No, you certainly don't, but if you've got nothing to hide, why wouldn't you?"

Ellen smiled smugly. "Your fairytales are nothing more than nasty industry gossip. But they mean nothing. I was nowhere near where Bunny Frank was murdered. I wasn't in town. I wasn't even in California. I was in Phoenix judging a dog show."

I took out a pen and notebook. "When did you leave LA and when did you get to Phoenix? Did you stay overnight or was it a day trip?"

I scribbled her itinerary as she laid it out. "I took the last flight out of LAX at ten forty-five and got into Phoenix at midnight. The dog show was an all-day event the next day. I took a flight back at eight-thirty and got to LA at ten."

"So, you were still in LA when Bunny was murdered. Did you share your schedule with the police?"

Ellen held out her hand. "I'll take the check now." She opened her office door. "I hate to cut this short, but I've got a new client meeting to prepare for."

****

My brain was on overload from my conversation with Ellen Thomas. Scenarios exploded inside my head like fireworks on the fourth of July. Ellen had samples from each swimwear supplier hanging in her office. With access to a Gotham swimsuit and shipping tape the entire industry uses, Ellen had the means. Now, she had the motive and the opportunity.

I stopped at A Jolt of Java for a shot of caffeine to clear the cobwebs. I paid for my cuppa and searched for an open chair. Louis Chennault was seated at a table in the back corner reading the West Coast Apparel News classified ads.

There was no other way to describe his appearance. The guy was a train wreck. He had two black eyes, one swollen half shut, the other winked on and off like a light bulb on the way out. His broken nose dangled like a baited fishing hook with its tip resting on his right cheek. He had a fat lower lip, and from the odd way his lips were set he had to be missing some teeth. His shattered left cheekbone was sunken in and cratered the side of his face, so even though he was facing straight ahead, it looked like a silhouette.

I stopped at his table and, without being invited, I took a seat across from him. Louis folded the paper and batted a greeting with the eye with the nervous tic. His speech was garbled, like he was talking with marbles in his mouth. "Come to exthamine the weckage?" His laugh was mocking. "Mobid curiosity is wather unbecoming."

I shook my head. "On the contrary. I could use some advice."

Louis waved the want ads under my nose and laughed sardonically. "If you need caweer advice, by all means, I'm your guy."

I took a sip of coffee and waited for a beat. "I'm investigating Bunny's murder and I'd like your take on who might have done it."

Louis poked a bony finger into his chest. "Since your number one suspect is no wonger in the wunning?"

I smiled contritely. "Yeah, something along those lines. Any pearls of wisdom on who Bunny pushed over the edge?"

Louis motioned to the mart lobby. "Take your pick. It could have been anyone." He tore the classified ads page out and crumpled the rest of the newspaper into a ball. "What do they say? Fowow the money and who had the most to wose?"

I laughed out loud. "Then you should still be sitting in jail."

"Twue enough. Except I had an alibi." He steepled his fingers. "Life is a twadeoff." He quirked a fatalistic smile. "It's not the end of the world. There will always be another woman and another gig."

What did Bunny Frank ever see in this jerk? "You had an alibi, but the word of a married woman you were having an affair with? How much credibility does a woman have who had to be threatened with jail before she backed your story?"

His laugh was nasty. "Enough for my get out of jail card. Do you want my vote? Wonnie Schwartzman. No one had more to wose." Louis unfolded his long legs and stood. "I'd better get going." He pressed his lips into a tight smile. "I've got some packing to do."

Louis warned, "I'd be careful asking Wonnie Schwartzman too many questions. Wonnie Schwartzman is a despoate man. Despoate men are dangerous. They have nothing weft to wose."

Yeah, like you.

Angela Wellborn walked past the barista station and came over to our table. She wrapped her arm around Louis' waist. Her glare could have melted a snowman. "See? Told ya. You were wrong."

Louis pushed in his chair and they disappeared into the crowded lobby.

I replayed our conversation and considered Louis Chennault's warning. Was he speaking from experience or was he a wise man? It wouldn't be long before I found out.

Chapter Twenty-Nine

"I've been doing some more nosing around." When I finished addressing the yentas, I surveyed the table. "Where does this leave us? Ellen Thomas was in LA at the time of Bunny's murder, and Sue Ellen and Leticia Lapidus have alibis. Sue Ellen was in San Diego and Leticia was at her kids' open school night. The cops aren't interested in Ronnie, and Louis has been cleared. So, if Angela, Michael, and Sandra Frank all have alibis, we're out of suspects. The police have run the entire swimwear industry through the system and got no hits. If you've never been in trouble with the law, your fingerprints aren't in the system. There's no way to compare yours to those at the crime scene."

Sonia tapped her lip. "Not entirely true. If you were in the military, your fingerprints and DNA are on file."

What was the chance of Sue Ellen Magee ready at dawn, decked out in camouflage, and taking orders from a drill sergeant to march in parade formation? Oh yeah; when elephants fly.

Sonia read my mind. "The same thing goes for a buyer. Most stores now require candidates to pass a drug test and provide a set of fingerprints before they are offered a job. Bunny and I had to comply at Hoffman's. The job level didn't matter; stock clerk or CEO, there was no option. If you refused, you were no longer under consideration."

Queenie's tone was incredulous. "You're saying buyers have to submit to those requirements or they don't get hired?'

Sonia said, "Every major store requires it."

Queenie wrinkled her nose as if she'd taken a whiff of yesterday's garbage. "Sounds pretty darned intrusive if you ask me."

Sonia shrugged. "Management's take is if you won't submit to it, you've got something to hide."

Joan blew out her cheeks. "Glad I'm on our side of the table."

Queenie gave Joan the stink eye. "Why? You got something to hide?"

Joan held out her hands. "No. I'm only saying it's nice there's a level of trust on our side."

Sonia smiled like an indulgent parent. "I hate to burst your bubble, but it's merely a matter of time till the wholesale side adopts the same hiring requirements. The potential liability is too much for vendors to ignore. Manufacturers can try fighting it, but ultimately there will be no choice. Retailers will demand suppliers take the same steps as they do to ensure their employees are clean. Several publicly traded apparel companies already require a drug test. Fingerprints can't be far behind."

Hope asked, "Is it a requirement for buying office buyers too?"

Sonia said, "All the major stores require it before they'd sign with the office."

I pressed the on- button of my cell. "I better give Martinez a call."

Chapter Thirty

I had an appointment to meet with Bunny's sister right before the dinner hour. Traffic into Beverly Hills would be pretty heavy. I called it a day to ensure enough travel time.

Dot Swimwear was the only showroom on the aisle not dark. I did a doubletake. The big room was empty. I opened the door as Michael Rothman hefted an overflowing carton and shoved it between two other boxes on the bottom of a packed rolling rack. If they were moving, I was curious as to where. No vacancies were available anywhere on the eleventh floor. "Michael, you guys moving to a bigger space?"

Michael's laugh was as hollow as an empty bottle. "Hardly. We're moving to the fifth floor."

"The children's wear floor?"

Michael studied his shoelaces. "Yeah."

"You guys getting out of swimwear?"

Michael hung his head. "Business is tough, and our showroom is too expensive. My boss Mark's older brother is a kids-wear rep. He has a big showroom, and he's letting us use part of it. All we have to pay for is our phones."

Michael stiffened when I hugged him. "I'm sorry the rumors were true. We're gonna miss you here on the aisle."

Michael smiled tightly. "Sometimes you don't get what you pay for."

"What do you mean?"

He forced the words out through clenched teeth. "I invested heavily with some individuals, and I didn't get the return on my investment I should have."

I gave him a sideways glance. "Paying off Bunny didn't pay off?"

He huffed, "I have no idea what you mean."

I didn't want to rip the guy a new one, especially when he was down on his luck. But patience with fools and liars has never been one of my strong suits. "Come on, Michael; don't yank my chain. Queenie Levine and I were two cars over from yours the first night of the swimwear market. Bunny Frank shook you down for a bucket of bucks."

He had the grace to blush. "She promised eight of our styles would make her must-buy list, but only one did. It's a small industry. It doesn't take much for the word to get around. It's devastating when a supplier doesn't get a good review from a major buying office who controls a lot of stores."

I gave him the big eyes. "You're blaming your bad season all on Bunny Frank?"

He dipped a shoulder. "We might have been thrown out of a few stores all on our own." He spat the anger out like a wad of chewing tobacco. "But Bunny's knife in the back opened the door. It gave a lot more stores the excuse they needed to shove us out."

"Where were you the night Bunny was murdered?"

Instead of answering, Michael pushed the rolling rack to the door and switched off the lights. "I wish I could hang around and chat more, but I've got to turn the key in before the mart office closes or they're gonna charge us for another month's rent." He checked the time. "I've got five minutes." He locked the door and pushed the rack to the elevator bank.

Had Bunny Frank finally pushed Michael Rothman beyond his limits? First Ronnie Schwartzman threw me out of his office. Now Michael Rothman did the same thing. An innocent man shines a light on the truth, he doesn't conceal it. I was determined to find out what they were working so hard to hide.

****

Sandra Frank might have been wheelchair-bound, but the pink-haired, sassy older version of her sister Bunny was no helpless invalid. She popped a wheelie on her motorized wheelchair as she welcomed me into the ground-level unit of the Spanish-style duplex she and Bunny inherited from their parents. Sandra laughed at my shocked expression. "Not all handicapped people are the guests of honor at pity parties."

Not exactly broken up nor particularly surprised by Bunny's murder, Sandra said she loved her sister because she was her sister, but she didn't like her. Sandra claimed she was Bunny's feel-good project. By fulfilling her promise to their parents to take care of her poor, crippled sister, Bunny absolved herself from all the rotten things she had done. Maybe Sandra got tired of being Bunny's shiny object?

Sandra's "caregiver" was a drop-dead gorgeous boy-toy and each other's alibi for the night of the murder. Sandra obviously couldn't have pulled off the murder on her own. But if she made a deal with the boy-toy to split the proceeds of her sister's sizeable estate, Bunny's sole heir could have convinced him to do the deed. Murder by checkbook anyone?

****

The next day I was ready to break for lunch when Detective Martinez walked into the showroom. "I got your message. You have some important information?" He took a notebook out of his jacket pocket and poised his pen, ready to write. "Anytime you're ready."

I took my purse out of the desk drawer. "You hungry, Detective? I was on my way out for a bite."

Martinez patted his stomach. "Starved. I got a late start this morning and skipped my usual oatmeal. The swill they call coffee at the station and a stale donut doesn't get you too far."

"There are a lot of dining choices around here. Anything particular tickles your fancy?"

Martinez shrugged. "I'm not picky. This is your neck of the woods. Why don't you surprise me?"

"You in the mood for Chinese food?"

Martinez grinned. "I'm always in the mood for Chinese food."

I was beginning to like this guy.

I clapped and smiled. "Then, Detective, you're in for a treat. One of the old-line joints from Chinatown recently opened a second location two blocks from the mart. If we hustle, we'll get there ahead of the lunch crowd. Blue China Moon has the best moo shoo this side of Beijing."

Once the waiter cleared the table, Martinez took his pen and notebook out of his jacket. "Your helpful information?" He narrowed his eyes. "Weren't you going to leave the detecting to the detective?"

I tried not to squirm in my seat. I went with as much truth as I could without getting into more hot water. "I am leaving the detecting to the detective. But I work right in the middle of your investigation. Let's face it; flashing a badge makes some folks, even the innocent ones, nervous enough to clam up. They all know me, and I'm a lot less intimidating than you. It stands to reason people might say things to me they might not say to you."

I took it as a tacit agreement when he dipped his head and didn't bite off mine. He opened his notebook and filled it.

I finished and cocked a brow. "So, Detective?"

My blush betrayed me when he said, "There's probably a lot more you haven't told me." He tapped the notebook with his pen. "But it sounds like I've got some follow-up interviews to schedule."

Chapter Thirty-One

I was on a deadline to finish the quarterly sales projection by the end of the week. I worked till the figures blurred together and called it a day. I wasn't anywhere close to being finished, so I brought my laptop home. A food break would revitalize my vision. It's a well-known fact pizza and ice cream are widely accepted as proven concentration enhancements.

This late, the parking structure only had a handful of cars scattered across the bottom level. I was halfway to the mustang when the hairs on the back of my neck inexplicably stood on edge. I attributed it to overwork, shook off the feeling, and kept going. I walked a few hundred yards more when the unmistakable sound of heavy footsteps behind me got my full attention. I quickened my pace and tried to stay calm. The footsteps got louder as they got closer. I increased my stride, but the footsteps were closing the distance between us at a furious pace. My heart banged so hard against my ribcage, miraculously, I didn't crack a couple of bones. I made an effort to slow my breathing from a pant to something closer to normal.

I slipped my fingers inside my purse. Where the heck was the can of mace my dad insisted I carry? Mental head slap. I changed purses to a smaller one two days ago and couldn't fit the canister in. Marvelous. My fingers were slick with perspiration as I pulled the keychain out of the inside pocket. The fob slipped out of my hand and fell to the bottom of the purse. It took several tries until I pulled the chain out. I tightened my hold on the strap of the laptop case. Not exactly an arsenal of weapons, but besides my wits and fleet feet, they were all I had.

Finally, the mustang was a hundred yards away. I resisted the urge to break into a sprint. I slipped the key into the door lock when a strong hand grabbed my shoulder from behind and something cold and hard jabbed into my lower back. Instinctively, I raised my hands. If this was a mugging, the mugger was gonna be pretty disappointed. All I had in my wallet was a twenty and two nearly maxed-out credit cards. I dropped the purse strap off my shoulder and held the bag behind my back. "I don't have much in my wallet, but take it all. Please don't hurt me."

"I don't want your money." A deep male voice commanded, "If you don't want to get hurt, don't do anything stupid."

I never excelled in doing what I was told. I tightened my grip on the keychain. The one thing I had in my favor was the element of surprise. I whirled around, widened my stance, ready to fight. I bounced on the balls of my feet and went for his eyes.

Who was my attacker? Louis Chennault? Michael Rothman? Ronnie Schwartzman? Jack the Ripper? Not even close. Osborne Bradley, CEO of Acme, the oldest and most prestigious buying office in the apparel industry certainly wasn't the first choice on my list. For an older guy, nothing was wrong with his reflexes. He held his muscular arms out and blocked my play. He snatched the keys out of my hand and growled, "I don't want to hurt you, but we need to talk."

I made a move for the keychain, but he held it over my head. "Behave and you'll get them back. You don't, enjoy the walk home."

The upper crust class oozed right out of Osborne Bradley's pores. In his early sixties, he had a mane of thick white wavy hair any woman with a pulse would pay a king's ransom to run her fingers through. He had wideset, piercing blue eyes above thin lips and a patrician nose. He was tall and trim with an athletic build. He wore an expensive, perfectly fitting hand-tailored suit. But right then, he wasn't too high class or uppercrust. He had the menacing sneer of a low-class hitman out for blood. Mine.

I tried not to stare at the gun, but my eyes had a mind of their own. Hopefully, snark masked the quiver of fear in my voice. "Normally, when one wants to talk, one calls and makes an appointment."

"What I have to say is best done in private."

I glared at the small-caliber pistol aimed at my chest. "Why? You don't want any witnesses?"

He leaned in and invaded my space. He stood close enough I could smell his expensive cologne. If he was trying to intimidate me, he was doing a darned good job. Dad's voice flitted around my brain. Don't show fear. Gee, Dad, thanks for the great advice. Too bad my knees won't stop knocking with the guy pointing a gun at my heart.

I sidestepped Bradley and backed up to get out of his reach, but the mustang was in the way. There was nowhere for me to go. Bradley was so close I could guess the flavor of his breath mint. I was trapped. Time to throw in the towel. I threw my arms out and waved around the deserted parking lot. "You wanna talk? The stage is yours. Knock yourself out."

He poked his long index finger under my nose and snarled, "Listen to me, you wise-ass punk. You're way out of your league tangling with me. I'm not gonna stand by and let you destroy an empire my grandfather built from nothing."

Whoa. I squinted my confusion. "You sure you have the right person? Frankly, I'm surprised you even know who I am."

He growled from the back of his throat. "I hear you're smart so don't play dumb with me."

I still had no idea what his problem was, but I wasn't going to make it easy for this stuffed shirt imitating James Cagney. "You're the one with the problem; spit it out already."

"Ellen Thomas told me your preposterous insinuations."

I jutted my jaw. "Facts are facts."

Bradley's face turned red as an overripe tomato. "You're a liar. You insinuated Ms. Thomas and I are romantically involved. You insinuated either I directed Ellen to murder Bunny Frank, or to prove her love for me Ellen did it all on her own."

"Several people overheard Ellen profess her undying love to you and declare there was nothing she wouldn't do to prove it." I slitted my eyes. "Maybe she did."

Bradley scoffed, "Utterly absurd. Never happened. Besides, I can't control Ellen's feelings for me. Trust me, they are not reciprocated. I'm a happily married man." He puffed out his chest. "Married to the same woman for twenty-five years." He snapped, "Happily married until you stuck your nose into my life."

Huh?

"Thanks to you, Detective Martinez came to my home and questioned me in front of my wife." Bradley put his free hand behind him and rubbed the small of his back. "No matter how many times I deny Ellen and I are involved, my wife isn't buying it."

Poor baby. Been spending the nights on the couch?

"Where there's smoke there's fire."

Bradley groaned. "Things were already bad enough with Bunny Frank bleeding us dry before you inserted yourself into our business. The horrid woman poached our biggest clients and stole a third of them. Since you sicced the cops on us, we're hemorrhaging accounts like a hemophiliac. The police have been in our office for days going through our files for who knows why. Somehow, word got out, and it spooked what's left of our customers. Yesterday we lost Diamond's, our oldest account. Jethro Barnes claimed they couldn't be associated with a company being investigated by the police. Some rubbish of not wanting the cops on their doorstep next. We've already lost twenty-five accounts, and fifteen others are one step from out the door. At this rate, we'll be out of business before the end of the year."

I stared perplexed at the man through curious eyes. "What do you want from me?"

Bradley spoke through clenched teeth. "You're going to make this right. You're gonna call off the cop and tell him you were wrong."

As if. I shook my head no. "No way. If you're innocent, he's giving you the chance to prove it. If you're guilty, he'll find the proof, and you and Ellen are done."

Bradley's face turned the shade of eggplant. "Ellen said you'd never back down." His smile was evil as he raised the gun and cocked the hammer. "What a shame. Guess you're gonna be the victim of a mugging gone bad."

As he aimed the gun at my head, the loud screech of tires distracted Bradley and gave me the chance I needed. I swung my laptop case with all my might and hit him square in the family jewels. He dropped the gun and fell with a thud like a box of rocks. Bradley lay writhing on the ground holding his privates and vomited all over his expensive suit.

The gun skidded away, but I didn't take the time to find it. Time to get out of Dodge. I snatched the keys out of his hand. "Pity your fancy suit is ruined, Osborne. I doubt the cleaners can save it."

Chapter Thirty-Two

The Argonaut got it right. Tuesday night was indeed moonless. Marina del Rey was as dark as the inside of a witch's cauldron. The dim streetlights on Palawan Way offered so little illumination, if you weren't familiar with the marina layout, it would be easy to fall into the drink.

I stopped at my mailbox in the dockmaster's office before meeting Queenie. Nothing earthshattering. My boater's insurance renewal notice, the monthly slip rental bill from Porto Paloma Marina, a West Marine catalog, a bunch of throwaway ads, and the latest edition of The Argonaut. I tossed the ads and stuffed the newspaper, catalog, and two pieces of mail in my jacket pocket.

Ten-fifty-five. I had to hustle if I was gonna be on time. Queenie and I were meeting in front of my basin at eleven. With twenty boat slip basins on either side, Porto Paloma Marina was bisected by an enormous three-building apartment complex. The dockmaster's office was located on the lower level of the farthest apartment building from my basin. I took a shortcut through the parking structure and got to my basin at eleven on the nose. Queenie was already there, pacing in front of my gate dressed head to toe incognito black like a Ninja. Her hair was tucked into a black watchman's cap. Her hands were encased in black leather gloves, and she'd smeared black shoe polish or something on her face. The only thing not black was the whites of her eyes.

I gave her the once-over. "Considering the caper, your outfit is a little overkill." I smirked. "And by the way, blackface is rather politically incorrect."

She scoffed, "Don't be an idiot. I'm a burglar, not a bigot."

I pointed at the goop staining her face. "You're gonna have a helluva time getting shoe polish off of your face."

She sighed. "It's not shoe polish, you twit. It's theatrical make-up. My next-door neighbor Annabelle is a make-up artist at one of the studios. She gave me a packet. It washes off with soap and warm water." Queenie pulled a small plastic container out of her coat pocket. "So, Miss Paleface, want some smeared on your kisser?"

The moonless sky was black as a coal mine. "Nah. We can use extra light."

She stowed the plastic container in her pocket and asked, "What's the game plan?"

I pointed to the sidewalk separating the basins and Palawan Way. "We go two basins over to fifteen hundred and open the gate. Ronnie's boat is the big one at the end of the dock."

"How do you get into his basin? Isn't this a security marina?"

I waved my key. "It is. Fortunately, the key opens any basin gate in Porto Paloma Marina."

"Ronnie must lock such an expensive boat like it's Fort Knox?"

"We can get aboard. Getting into the inside of the cabin is the challenge. The cabin door will be locked."

Queenie patted her jacket pockets. “I don’t have a lock pick, and my nail file won’t do the trick. How do you plan to get inside? Wave a magic wand?”

“Boaters are creatures of habit. We all hide an extra key. I have an idea where he’d hide one.”

“And if the boat is alarmed?”

I grinned, “Then you better be a fast runner or know how to swim.”

“Is there a security guard?”

“There’s a rent-a-cop who makes the rounds at the top of the hour.” Time check. Eleven-fifteen. I pointed across the channel. “The guard begins at the first basin on the other side of those apartment buildings and makes his way around the entire complex. He starts his rounds at eleven o’clock. It takes an hour to go completely around the marina. If he doesn’t make any stops, he should be here in forty-five minutes.” I opened the gate and motioned her in. “Let’s be on the safe side and say a half-hour.”

We went down the gangplank onto the walkway. We got to Ronnie’s boat and Queenie’s eyes bugged. “Holy cow. Wasn’t the Queen Mary docked in Long Beach?” She studied Ronnie’s yacht from stem to stern. “I’m no boat expert, but a half hour’s not gonna do it.”

I said, “It’s a big boat, but the interior may be compact. This time we’ll split up.” I climbed the five steps at midship. I unzipped the clear Plexiglas enclosure and tied it back. I slipped through the opening and waved Queenie aboard. I untied the enclosure and zipped it closed from the inside so as not to appear out of place to anyone else on the dock. I jiggled the handle on the cabin door. Naturally, locked. Queenie pursed her lips. “Now what?”

I did a one-eighty around the deck. "Now let's find out if Ronnie hides an extra key like the rest of us do."

Queenie asked, "Can I help?"

"Yeah. It'll go a lot faster with two of us searching." I discounted the pull-out drawers below the wheel well. "Those drawers are too obvious. It's the first place anyone would check."

The seating area was a series of canvas cushions in a horseshoe around the deck. "My next-door neighbor Mark hides his spare key inside one of his cushions. Let's start there. You start at the port end, and I'll take the starboard. We'll meet in the middle." From her blank expression, I might as well have been speaking Urdu. "You take the left side and I'll take the right. Unzip the cushions and feel around under the foam." I showed her my key fob. "The key will most likely be on a floatable rubber fob like mine."

I opened the third cushion when the high beam headlights of a slow-moving car lit up Ronnie's boat like a lighthouse beacon. Was the rent-a-cop now patrolling by car or worse; had one of Ronnie's neighbors noticed us and called the cops? Cripes. I whisper-yelled a warning. "Get down!" We dropped to the deck on our bellies like a couple of flounders and waited till the car passed. We squandered precious minutes we didn't have to spare waiting till the car drove onto Admiralty Way.

Queenie tapped a finger over her chest. "We better find the key in the next five minutes or I'm outta here. My ticker's ready to explode."

We worked our way around to the center of the horseshoe. Queenie opened the sixth cushion and stuck her hand in. She waved the key like a winning lottery ticket. She squealed a lot louder than I wish she had. "OMG. You are brilliant."

I silently thanked Mark and took a bow.

Eleven-twenty. Palawan Way was still deserted. No one on the gangplank or the walkway. So far, so good. We straightened the cushions back to their original places in case someone walked on the dock. I slipped the key in and unlocked the cabin door. I closed it behind us and locked it from the inside. No alarm keypad next to the door. Curious. Hopefully, it wasn't hidden in a secret spot or worse, a silent alarm. Too late now. In for a penny, in for a pound. We'd find out soon enough.

The Bikini Mistress was laid out like most luxury yachts; all rooms were off the main salon. The galley was on the port side and featured a full-size kitchen with a built-in breakfast nook roomy enough to seat a baseball team.

The den was starboard and had floor-to-ceiling filled bookshelves, a big-screen TV, and a pool table. Next to the den was one of three full-size heads (bathrooms). A small V-berth, two small bedrooms, and the second head were in succession next to the den. One of the bedrooms was equipped as an office. The master bedroom suite was at the aft end (back) and featured two walk-in closets, and a king-size bed and matching dressers. The head had a stall shower, a full bathtub, and a jacuzzi.

This wasn't a boat. This was a floating palace. Good to be king.

Queenie asked, "How do you wanna do this?"

"Start with the master suite and work your way back. Closets and dressers first, if there's time, check under the mattresses. When you're finished with the master, do all the small bedrooms and the V-berth. Start with the one equipped like an office. I'll take the galley, the two additional heads, the main salon, and the engine room below. Be thorough but tidy. The place is neat as a pin. No time to go back and straighten things. Do it as you're going. We can't leave any clues someone's been here nosing around."

She asked, "What am I looking for?"

A smoking gun would be dandy. "Something incriminating. You'll know it when you see it."

Besides a variety of gourmet food in the fridge and a well-stocked wine cellar, the galley was a big nothing burger. Not so much as a crumb between the breakfast nook cushions. The heads and linen closet proved to be another disappointment. All the furniture in the main salon was covered in plastic. Either it had never been used or it had been recently delivered.

So far, this entire adventure was a waste of time. The engine room was my last shot. I climbed the narrow ladder into the cavernous darkness. I hit the flashlight app on my phone and beamed it around. The Bikini Mistress had huge twin diesel engines big enough to power an aircraft carrier. The number of valves, gauges, and wires rivaled a seven-forty-seven. My humble houseboat, by comparison, has a single thirty horsepower outboard engine I've never used.

I twisted sideways and crept across the narrow walkway separating the two engines. I was afraid to touch anything above the engine mounts. Three storage cabinets were below each of the engines. I got on my knees and shined my flashlight inside. Nothing but spare parts.

Defeated, I climbed back to the main deck. Maybe Queenie had better luck. If not, I was out of ideas. I closed the hatch and almost jumped out of my skin. Queenie bounced on her heels in front of me. "What the heck have you been doing all this time?"

I gave her the stink eye. "Square dancing. Why? Did you find anything?"

She shook her head no. "It took forever to search, but except for his wife's kinky lingerie, there was nothing out of the ordinary in the master suite. I didn't get to the V berth or the other bedrooms yet. What do you want me to do next?"

My watch decided for us. "Forget the other bedrooms and V berth. The office is the important one. Let's go through it together. I'll take the desk. You take the closet."

The computer and printer took up most of the space on the small walnut desk. Charts and maps in the top drawer. Files of major accounts, line lists, and color brochures in the bottom one. Nothing incriminating. Dang.

I was ready to call it a night when Queenie's muffled voice called out, "Hey, I've got something."

She came out of the closet holding a towel with an icepick, a pair of blood-stained cutting shears, and a roll of shipping tape with a big section unevenly cut off all wrapped inside. She held out her other hand. "This was under the roll of tape. Any idea what it is?"

My heart jumped to my throat. She was holding my distributor cap. Queenie said, "Ronnie's personal belongings were moved from his office closet to this one." She held out the towel. "I found all this hidden inside a pocket in his golf bag. Shouldn't we give all this stuff to Detective Martinez?"

I shook my head no. "We can't take it with us. If we do, it would break the chain of possession and we can't prove we found it on Ronnie's boat." I opened the camera app on my phone. "Put them on the desk and I'll take some photos. After I finish, maybe we can find Ronnie's marine license. We can photograph the license next to all this stuff. The date and time stamp will prove they were on Ronnie's boat."

I aimed the camera and kept shooting. "If this doesn't convince Martinez Ronnie did it, nothing will." The flash from the camera lit the small room like a klieg light. I'd taken my last shot when a blinding light shined in through the porthole. Crap. Neither Nancy Drew nor Miss Marple remembered to cover the porthole. We dived under the desk as the beam of light passed over the porthole again.

A man's voice called out, "Mr. Schwartzman, this is George from security. Are you on board?"

Eleven-forty-eight. Our luck, George was a lot faster on his feet than Ernesto. The light beam passed over the porthole again.

Queenie's voice cracked, "What if he comes onto the boat?"

Indeed, what if?

I stopped breathing altogether with the sound of the enclosure being unzipped. The boat was tied securely, but it rocked enough to jostle us out from under the desk when George stepped onto the deck. I whispered back, "He opened the Plexiglas enclosure the same way as me and got on the deck. But I locked the door from the inside." I waved Ronnie's key. "He has no way to get inside the interior of the boat."

George rattled the locked door handle and called out. "Mr. Schwartzman, are you ok?"

Queenie whispered, "Bet the camera flash got his attention."

I whispered, "Absolutely."

She shook like a leaf in a rainstorm. "What do we do?"

"Stay here till he disembarks and goes on with the rest of his rounds. Hopefully, he didn't call the cops." I crawled over to the porthole and snuck a quick peek. A light shone from one of the apartments across from the marina. "If we're lucky, he'll assume the flash inside the boat was a reflection of the light coming from one of the apartments across the street."

The boat rocked from side to side as George walked around the deck. He tapped his nightstick along the transom and opened and closed the storage bins. Thank God we put the deck cushions back. After an eternity, George secured the enclosure and got off the boat. He beamed his flashlight into the bedroom a few more times, and finally he hit the walkway. But until the security gate clanked shut, my heart didn't leave my throat.

I said, "Forget Ronnie's license. The boat will rock too much with both of us roaming around trying to find it. We can't take the chance the guard decides to come back for a second inspection. Put this stuff back where you found it and let's wait fifteen minutes. If the boat isn't swarming with cops, let's boogie."

She said, "You do what you want, but I'm telling you now if it gets ugly, I'm not jumping off any boat into gunky water." Queenie shivered. "I'll take my chances with the cops."

I smiled grimly. "If George called the cops, Rose Markowitz better be accepting new clients."

****

I got onto my boat around twelve-thirty and counted my blessings. I pulled the mail out and put it on the galley table. The insurance bill, the catalog, and The Argonaut were there but not the slip rental bill. Crap. I checked my pants pockets, shirt, jacket, and for the heck of it, inside my bra and panties. The bill was nowhere. I mentally retraced my departure steps from the evening of fun and frolics. If the bill slipped out of my jacket when we jumped off the boat, it could be half-way to Hawaii by now. I wrote a note to myself to call the Marina office the next day for a duplicate bill. I fell into bed and was asleep before my head hit the pillow.

Chapter Thirty-Three

It had been a long, challenging day. Delivery problems, pissy customers, cranky sales reps. Even a Thai Chicken pizza didn't improve this stinker of a day. The best part of this one? Finito. I stretched over the transom and put my briefcase on the forward deck. I held the guard rail and hoisted one leg over. I almost fell overboard when Ronnie Schwartzman popped out of the shadows.

"Ronnie," I croaked as I straddled the deck. "What the heck is the matter with you? You scared the crap outta me." I hauled my leg over the edge and pointed to the murky water. "I almost fell into the drink."

Ronnie tsked, "Gee, would have been such a shame."

The guy was a total putz.

Ten-fifteen. Pretty late for a social call. "Why are you at the marina on a school night?"

For once, not having a well-lit dock was a blessing. He couldn't see the color drain from my face when he waved my slip rental bill in front of my nose.

His tone was deceptively conciliatory, but the evilness of his smile froze the blood in my veins. "Being a good neighbor and hand-delivering this to you."

I took a few beats to gather my wits and managed to come up with a plausible comeback. "Geez, I'm sorry if the mailman put it in your box by accident. It happens all the time. The two names are close but the carrier must be a blind guy. I get a ton of stuff not belonging to me for anyone else whose last name starts with an S."

"Nope, the mailman didn't put it in the wrong box."

"You found it on the street?"

"Wrong. Keep guessing."

"Parking structure?"

"Guess again."

I smiled, "It doesn't matter where you found it, I'm just glad you did." I made a showing of a jaw-cracking yawn. "I'd invite you in for a drink, but it's late and I've got an early day tomorrow." I waggled my fingers. "So, let me have the envelope and I'll say good night."

He rolled the envelope between his fingers but made no move to hand it over. Was he waiting for a reward? It wouldn't surprise me. "Listen, I appreciate you going to the trouble of hand-delivering it. I'd hate to pay a late fee. Tomorrow lunch is on me."

Ronnie growled like a grizzly. "I told you to guess again." Out of guesses, I kept my yip shut, but an involuntary shudder crept the length of my spine when he snarled, "Do it."

The tang of his sweat mixed with his cologne filled my nostrils. I edged to the back of the deck. "Ronnie," I said in a calm voice not sounding anything like mine. "I can't guess. I don't have any idea."

He mimicked me. "You don't have any idea?" He held the envelope above my head.

Was he going to make me jump for it? I wouldn't put it past him.

"No clue." I eyed the guard rail, ready to do a Tarzan imitation and swing back onto the dock. I slid to the far edge of the deck. He stayed with me. I slid back to the spot where I was before, and he was right there. We danced the slow shuffle samba around the deck three times. "Ronnie, this isn't your big boat. It's a small deck. Move back a little will ya?"

Instead, he came even closer and waved the envelope in my face. I tried to snatch it, but he was too fast. He dangled it over the water. "Wanna know where I found this?" When I didn't answer, he thundered, "On the engine room floor on my boat!"

A few of my neighbor's interior lights blinked on. I silently blessed our close quarters.

He spat out the words like seeds from an orange. "Now how do you suppose it got there?"

I lifted a shoulder. "No idea."

"How else? You were on my boat."

I shrank back as he hovered over me. Jack from the beanstalk versus the giant. Cripes.

I channeled my dad and stuck out my chin. "Are you nuts?"

He said, "The security guard reported a light on inside my boat Tuesday night. I haven't been on board for over a week."

"And how am I responsible? Maybe there's an electrical short. Did you check the fuse box?"

He raised his eyebrows. "You burgled my showroom. No surprise you burgled my boat."

I folded my arms across my chest and struck an indignant pose. "And how did I manage to get into your boat?"

He fingered the Plexiglas enclosures surrounding my deck. "Easy. You unzipped the enclosure like this one and boarded."

I asked, "Don't you lock it? An expensive boat like yours, isn't it alarmed?"

He waved his key fob in my face. "You searched around, probably had an idea where to find the extra key, and let yourself inside."

For someone who wasn't there, he did a darned good job of describing exactly what I'd done. His shriek bounced off my houseboat and echoed around the dockside like an amusement park funhouse. "I warned you to keep outta my way, but you didn't listen. Now you're gonna pay."

I gauged my chances. The murky channel wasn't an option, and I'd never get the mace out of my purse in time. Weapons? Not a one except my brain and my mouth.

"What are you gonna do, Ronnie? Kill me like you killed Bunny?"

"I didn't kill her." Ronnie snarled, "Miserable Limey Chennault beat me to it."

I scoffed, "You wish. Unlike you, he had an actual alibi."

Ronnie huffed, "So he says."

Foolishly, I taunted him. "Did you bring any packing tape with you?"

Ronnie hissed, "Shut up."

Like a moron, I egged him on. "Bring any bikinis to jam into my mouth? Can I pick which print goes best with my outfit?"

"You can't stop your yammering, can ya?" Ronnie's eyes glittered. "Why don't I do the world a big favor and shut you up once and for all?" He lunged and swung a ham-sized hand to shove me into the channel. I swatted his hand away, but his fingertips burned my face when they grazed my cheek. He made another grab for my arm. I jumped out of the way, but he tripped me. He lifted me off the deck by the scruff of my shirt. I leaned back against the rim of the deck and pushed off with my arms. I got some leverage and bent my knees. I aimed for his crotch, but with my short legs the angle was off. The arc of the kick wasn't high enough, and I only tapped his kneecaps.

He dangled me over the water and swung me around. I let out a blood-curdling scream loud enough for all my liveaboard neighbors to run onto their decks. Mark, the hulking ex-Navy seal whose trawler was moored in the slip next to mine, leaped over his deck to my boat wearing nothing but his boxers. Mark landed on my deck, and Ronnie dropped me under the transom like a sack of potatoes.

As big as Ronnie Schwartzman was, Mark easily dwarfed him. Graceful for a big man, Mark got between Ronnie and me. Mark waved his baseball-bat-sized arm around at all our neighbors and sneered. "Hey, Mr. Macho tough guy, why don't you pick on someone your own size?" Mark jabbed a sausage-sized finger into Ronnie's chest. "Let's see how tough you are when the playing field is level."

Ronnie backed up and held out his hands in supplication. He waved my envelope in front of him like a white flag. He stammered, "H-hey m-man, I-I don't want any trouble." He shoved the envelope into my hands. "I got this by accident and came to deliver it." Ronnie kept his hands in the air and edged over to the end of the deck.

Ronnie leaned over and whispered, "This isn't over, sister; not by a long shot. Better keep an eye over your shoulder. I'm warning you. Stay off my boat, stay outta my office, and stay outta my life. If not, bad things are gonna happen." He jutted his chin at Mark. "Next time your big goon might not be around to save you."

Ronnie took hold of the guard rail and hoisted himself over the deck. He jumped onto the dock and graced Mark with an aw-shucks you caught me grin. He held out his hands. "Didn't mean anything. I'll be going now." He ran up the gangplank and charged through the gate like his boxers had caught fire.

I gushed, "Mark, what would I have done without you? You saved my bacon. I owe you big time."

Mark bounced on the balls of his feet and quirked an embarrassed smile. "Nah, I didn't do anything special. You don't owe me anything." Mark pointed to Ronnie's disappearing backside. "My blood boils when a big lummox like him can only make himself feel like a he-man by threatening a woman. His mama should have raised him better. Jerks like him have to be taught manners." Mark grinned. "From the mess of the guy's face, somebody beat me to it."

I patted my cheeks. "Believe it or not, the other guy was a lot worse." Mark was so tall, I had to bend backward to see his face. "Is it too late for a beer? You certainly earned it."

Mark laughed. "It's never too late for a beer." He put his big hands over the front of his boxers and blushed. "Let me go put my pants on."

Chapter Thirty-Four

The incident with Ronnie Schwartzman nagged at me like an itch I couldn't scratch. My dad taught his children never to start a fight, but always finish it. I couldn't let this slide. If I didn't let Bunny Frank, Sue Ellen Magee, or Angela Wellborn push me around, I certainly wasn't gonna let Ronnie Schwartzman.

I opened our showroom door and called over my shoulder to Hope. "I'll be back. I've got something to take care of." Nobody threatens Holly Schlivnik and gets away with it, even if he's a foot taller and outweighs her by a hundred pounds.

Though no one manned the huge space, the Clothing Concepts door was unlocked. Curious. All the road reps were traveling but where were the assistants? Carrie Le Beau was at the Clothing Concepts factory, but where was Ronnie's assistant? Had Mitzi quit with the receptionist? Ronnie Schwartzman making coffee? Typing memos? Fat chance. I'd make a fortune selling tickets to that performance.

I called out, "Ronnie, it's Holly Schlivnik. We've gotta talk. Now." I waited for a beat or two. Nada. Nothing but dead air. Seriously? This is how he was gonna play it? If ignoring me was his game plan, he could kiss my grits. Still, my Nana always said you catch more flies with honey, so I tempered the annoyance in my voice. "Ronnie, it's Holly. I'm not going away, and neither is the situation. We need to settle this." Five beats. So much for temperance. Who was I kidding? Patience was never one of my strong points. I yelled, "Ronnie! For crying out loud, stop being such a jerk." Zippo response. I was talking to myself.

There was only one way in or out of the Clothing Concepts showroom, the door I came in through. Ronnie Schwartzman was no Spiderman. He wouldn't climb out a window and crawl eleven floors down. There was no way to escape. "Ronnie, you've gotta come out sooner or later and when you do, I'm gonna be here, so let's deal with this now and quit wasting time."

This was getting me nowhere fast. I cupped my hands around my mouth like a megaphone. "All right. You don't wanna come out? No problem. I'm coming in."

The door to Ronnie's office was closed. I was tempted, but I'd been raised better than to barge in uninvited. I put my ear against the door. A man's voice was talking, but it didn't sound like Ronnie's. Oddly, it sounded far away.

I rapped on the door three times and called his name one more time. "Ronnie?" Nothing. I rapped on the door again. The strange voice was still talking but I got no reply. Now he was a ventriloquist? I didn't have time for his childish games. Screw the niceties and the way I was raised. I was over it. I opened the door and stepped in. The TV was tuned to CNBC with Jim Cramer on "Mad Money." Much to my surprise, Ronnie wasn't seated behind his desk watching Cramer screaming like a lunatic over some hot stock.

A half dozen fashion magazines were strewn across the desk. A pair of blood-splotched cutting shears lay next to a glue stick on top of the magazines. The wastebasket was filled with bloody tissues, several Band-Aid wrappers, a blood-stained swimsuit, and the cut-out frames of the words used in the threatening letters.

All of Ronnie's clothes and suitcases were missing. Unless he was hiding in the closet, Ronnie Schwartzman was in the wind. I opened the closet for giggles and squeaks. Other than a couple of naked hangers, the closet was empty. Ronnie Schwartzman was gone. Had he been fired and didn't care if he left the showroom wide open? If he didn't get canned, where the heck was he?

Was Louis still around? I rapped on his office door. "Louis, it's Holly Schlivnik. I need to talk to you." Nothing. I'd had it with these two pretentious jerks yanking my chain. Ronnie was history, but Louis was a different story. I had no intention of letting him slip through my fingers. I opened his office door a crack and squinted in. The lights were off, and the windowless office was pitch dark. I opened the door wider and craned my neck for a better view. A silhouetted figure sat behind the desk. Why didn't he answer? Was he asleep or merely born in a barn?

I found the switch behind the door and pressed the lights on. A dozen packed cartons were stacked along the left-side wall. "Louis…" The rest of the words stuck in my mouth. My eyes traveled from his battered face to his neck, and bile rose in the back of my throat. Several layers of the same tape Bunny Frank had been trussed with were wrapped tightly around Louis

Chennault's neck. A bloody Gotham swimsuit had been fashioned into a Windsor knot as though he was wearing a necktie. A macabre corpse going formal. His head was tilted back against the chair and was barely attached to his neck. If the tape had been cinched any tighter, he would have been decapitated.

Rivulets of blood had leaked out of his neck where the wire-like string embedded in the tape had cut into it. The blood had stained his white polo shirt the same pale shade of cotton candy-pink as my mustang. His distorted facial features were a mottled shade of eggplant. His swollen head was the size of an over-inflated balloon ready to explode.

His arms were bent at the elbows and were laid across his chest like crossed swords. His fingers were clamped around the handle of a coffee cup with a Gotham Swimwear insignia clutched in his palms to his chest. Murky dregs of stale coffee coated the bottom of the cup. His torso was bound to the chair by the same shipping tape wrapped around his neck.

The similarity between how both victims' bodies were posed was chilling. Decorated with a Gotham swimsuit, each corpse had a monstrous but telling signature. Screw the science; the science had to be wrong. I was no Sherlock Holmes, but from here in the bleachers, Ronnie Schwartzman was one corpse away from being tagged as a serial killer. First Bunny Frank, now Louis Chennault. Who was the next casualty on Ronnie Schwartzman's hit list? Queenie Levine? Sue Ellen Magee? Angela Wellborn? The haunting memory of Ronnie Schwartzman's threat made me shiver, and any vestiges of laughter died on my lips. I better pay attention, or the next victim might be me.

Chapter Thirty-Five

I returned to our showroom and called 911. I told the operator there was no rush. The victim wasn't in a big hurry. No need to blare the siren or blast through any red lights since nothing more could be done for Louis Chennault.

Either Detective Martinez was in the area or he had the scanner on. He walked in ten minutes later. We got to Louis' office door and Martinez snarked, "Touch anything this time?"

If he was goading me, I didn't take the bait. "The door handle and light switch."

Martinez donned a pair of thin latex gloves and pointed to the hallway. "Wait in the showroom. I have to talk to you but, first, I've gotta check this out."

Fifteen minutes later, the paramedics, Sophie Cutler, and her crew arrived. "Why am I not surprised to find you in the middle of all this?"

I was in no mood for her smart-alecky cracks, so I threw them right back. "Nice to see you too. Let's do lunch. Have your people call my people."

Like a tour guide, I directed the parade back to Louis' office. With all their equipment, the backup rivaled Friday night rush hour traffic on the Hollywood freeway.

Martinez emerged from Louis' office a half hour later. He pulled off the latex gloves and glared. "What is it with you, Ms. Schlivnik?" Martinez's eyes blazed with anger. "Are you determined to get yourself killed, or are you merely incapable of following directions?"

I should have mentioned Osborne Bradley and Ronnie, but I needed another lecture like I needed a bigger tush. I had enough of this cop and his attitude to last me a lifetime. "If you'd do your job," I fired back, "I wouldn't have to."

I waved towards the office complex. "Did you go into Ronnie's office while you were back there?" I didn't wait for an answer. "No? Don't waste time chastising me. Get in there. You'll find a pile of fashion magazines with pages cut out like the ones we found in Louis' office. Ronnie used them to make the threatening letters, and you chose to do absolutely nothing. The frames of the magazine cut-outs, a bunch of bloody tissues, a band-aid wrapper, and a blood-soaked swimsuit are in his wastebasket." I added an extra-large dollop of snark to my voice. "In case you missed it the day they covered it at the academy, those are called clues."

Martinez folded his arms across his chest. "Ms. Schlivnik…"

I spat, "Don't Ms. Schlivnik me, Detective, because I'm not interested. You won't find Ronnie's clothes in his office. Any idea what it means? It means he's gone. He's not guilty? An innocent man doesn't run. An innocent man sticks around to clear his name. If you'd paid any attention to me, Louis would still be alive. Louis Chennault's blood is on your hands, not mine."

I left without asking for permission. Was Martinez finished questioning me? I didn't know, I didn't care. I went back to the Ditzy showroom. Queenie showed up five minutes later and gave me the once-over. "No offense, but when were you hit by the bus?"

Nothing gets past you, Queenster.

She pulled my chair away from the desk and grabbed my purse out of the bottom drawer. "Come on, pal. Let's get you outta here. Chardonnay and a bowl of lobster ravioli are exactly what the doctor ordered."

****

It's a good thing Queenie and I are regular customers at Pasta at the Pier. Mario took one look at me, and the restaurant owner's eyes widened as big as pizzas. He took it upon himself to bring a bottle of Chianti and two glasses to the table. He patted my cheek and smiled. "Bella. I tinka you a needa dis."

Mario, you have no idea. I eyed the bottle. Does anyone mind if I chug it?

Mario uncorked the bottle and poured Queenie and me each a glass. He toasted us with the bottle and set it in the middle of the table. He grinned. "Donta worry. Ittsa onna di house."

By the time we finished our meal, we were the last customers still in the restaurant. The clock shaped like the map of Italy on the wall behind the bar showed ten-thirty. The staff had worked around us and sat at a back table waiting for us to leave. Guilt pinched my conscience. Mario came to our table. "You takka your time. You stay alla di night if you a wanna. You, two good customers, so Mario donta care." Mario lifted the empty bottle. "Ya wanta more Chianti?" The diamond embedded in his front tooth winked when he smiled at me. "Ittsa gonna helpa ya sleep. Mario, he bringa you whatever ya want." Mario was disappointed when we passed on the second bottle of Chianti. Not wanting to hurt his feelings, we settled for two coffees and split a cannoli. Queenie regarded me over the rim of her coffee cup. "Out with it already. It's way past my bedtime."

I blinked my confusion. "Out with what?"

She tsked. "Oh please; cut the crap. It's written all over your face. You've got something to say but you aren't sure you should say it."

I'd never make a living as a poker player. I'd telegraph every hand. When I finished, she choked, "My God, they could have killed you. Did you call the police? File a complaint?"

I stared into the coffee. "No."

"Martinez?"

"Nope."

She growled, "Before I throttle you, can you tell me why not?"

I shrugged, "Because there was no point."

She snapped, "Have you lost your mind?"

The way things were going, I probably had. "It's their word against mine. The parking garage was empty when Osborne accosted me. The guy in the car had no idea we were even there. He was driving too fast and was too far away. He was at the west exit and the opposite end of the parking lot from us. I'd have to guess at the car color; something dark is the best I could do. I couldn't tell you the make of the car, let alone a license plate number. There was nobody else."

Queenie's voice had an accusatory tone like I was the one who'd done something wrong. "And Ronnie? You had a whole dock full of witnesses to back up your story."

I blew out my cheeks. "No one witnessed the attack. My scream got them onto their decks, but it was after the fact. When Mark got there, Ronnie dropped me onto my deck." I touched the spot on my face where Ronnie's fingers had grazed my cheek. "Ronnie didn't even leave a mark."

Her eyes lasered me with a sear hot as a blowtorch. "Do you realize how lucky you are?"

An involuntary shudder crawled the length of my spine.

She smacked her palm on the table. "This poking around is nuts. We're giving Martinez what we've got, and then we're done snooping. Dead is forever. And by the way, you're staying at my place till they find Ronnie." I opened my mouth to object, and Queenie put her hand out like a traffic cop. "Listen before you say no. My two-car garage is attached. You come into the condo without having to go from your car into the dark street. The guest bedroom is completely private with a full bathroom. My next-door neighbors are two big burly bodybuilders who work out at Venice Beach. I feed Lucy and Ethel, their Rottweilers, when the two guys go out of town for bodybuilding contests. If I asked them to, one of those musclemen would sleep on my couch if we didn't feel safe. Your houseboat isn't exactly Fort Knox in the security department. Let's face it, I could break into it without much effort. My place has a state-of-the-art alarm system, but if an intruder did manage to break in, Sampson and Delilah would scratch their eyes out."

I smiled, "I appreciate the offer, but your two overly pampered Siamese cats aren't exactly ferocious security guards. Besides, I'm deathly allergic to cats. I can't be around them for more than five minutes before my eyes swell shut and I sneeze my brains out. If an intruder didn't get me, the cats would finish me off." I waved off her concerns with a twist of my wrist. "I promise to take all the precautions. The sliding glass door is double-locked with a pole jammed in the bottom for extra security. I have a deadbolt lock and always block the door handle of the front door with a chair at night. It's not an alarm system, but anyone who'd get in would fall on their faces. With the noise, there's some warning. I keep a baseball bat under the bed. I was a tomboy as a kid, and I've got a brother. I've had a lot of practice. I'm pretty good at swinging a bat. Anyone gets in, I won't hesitate to beat their brains into a pulp. I'll speak to the dockmaster tomorrow morning and ask for the security guard to patrol my boat a few extra times." I jutted my jaw. "I've gotta live my life or Osborne and Ronnie have already won."

****

Queenie's nagging was relentless. Remarkable how she could become such a pain in the ass when she put her mind to it. We met with Detective Martinez the next afternoon. Regrettably, I was right. Martinez listened to the stories and said I was welcome to file charges. But with he said/she said nature of the incidents, they were unlikely to stick.

We gave him the photos I'd taken on Ronnie's boat. Martinez could barely contain his annoyance. "These photos were taken during the commission of a crime." He glared at me. "Breaking and entering is against the law, so they're the fruit of a poisoned tree." He stroked his mustache. "I'll need my Captain to clear it first, but given Mr. Schwartzman's attack on you, there are one or two sympathetic judges who may accept the photos as probable cause and issue a search warrant."

On the way to my basin after work, I took a detour and walked over to where the Bikini Mistress was moored. The slip was empty. Had he taken a night cruise, or did Ronnie run?

Martinez called two days later, and the question was answered. The good news was he got the search warrant. The bad news was when he attempted to serve it, Ronnie Schwartzman had moved his boat out of Porto Paloma Marina. I told the detective to check the Del Rey Yacht Club. Martinez contacted the Coast Guard. The detective assured me Ronnie and his boat would be found. Would it be before Ronnie killed his next victim?

Chapter Thirty-Six

Forget achieving world peace, a cure for cancer, or even a huge order from Sue Ellen Magee. The only subject the yentas were interested in was murder. Within a week their questions had morphed from did you get it wholesale to when did you discover the body? Yikes. Familiarity does breed contempt.

Joan looked around the table. "Anyone catch the eleven o'clock news last night? Channel four sent out a Barbara Walters wannabe to do an in-depth investigative report on the crime wave plaguing the mart." Joan blew out her cheeks. "Listen to the reporter, and the building was the west coast headquarters of murder incorporated."

Sonia muttered, "A few more murders here and it will be."

Hope sighed. "This mess doesn't get cleared up soon, we can all stay home. There won't be a business left to come to."

Sonia's eyes widened like a kewpie doll. "What do you make of all the LAPD patrolling the mart?"

Queenie pointed at the barista station with two uniforms standing in line. "Martinez must have cleaned out the precinct. The place is loaded with wall to wall cops." The two uniforms took their coffees and panned the room. Queenie rolled her eyes. "Does Martinez actually think a killer is hiding in the mart?"

Joan said, "Ronnie's an arrogant jerk, but he's not stupid. If he's guilty, no way he's hanging around here. With his money, he's on the other side of the world by now." Joan dipped her head. "Not to speak ill of the dead, but with Louis out of the picture, the word at CC is unless she screws it up, Carrie Le Beau is likely getting a big promotion the easy way."

Hope's mouth gaped open wide enough to catch flies. "You suggesting she killed Louis to get his job?"

Joan made a sour face. "Of course not. Louis' game of smoke and mirrors eventually blew up in his face. When the truth came out, he was canned. Carrie will probably get his job since she was already doing it."

I said, "Joan's right. It can't be Carrie. She had no motive to kill Louis. And I doubt she ever met Bunny. These two murders are related. Stands to reason the same person killed them both. It's gotta be Ronnie. Who else is there? No one else had as much to lose."

Sonia asked, "Then is the deal sealed Ronnie killed them both?"

I shrugged. "If it looks like a duck and quacks like a duck, it's a duck. Louis and Ronnie both had plenty of motive. It looked like they worked together and killed Bunny, and things went off the rails. But there was a fly in the ointment. Louis had an alibi. Ronnie's another story. An innocent man sticks around to clear his name. If you're not guilty, you don't run away."

Queenie said, "Martinez better find Ronnie before Holly and me get bumped off next."

I waved her off. "Nah. Despite his threats, we're not the ones Ronnie's gonna go after next." I sent a silent prayer I was right. "Angela Wellborn is the one who should be sweating. Bunny, Louis, and Angela are the ones who created all of Ronnie's problems, not Queenie and me." Who was I trying to convince? The yentas or me? I smiled grimly. "Let's say Ronnie already took care of Bunny and Louis. Ronnie gets rid of Angela, and the scales are even." Despite my bravado, my knees were knocking like an untuned engine. Cripes. I tipped my head to the barista station as Angela Wellborn walked into A Jolt of Java. "Speak of the devil."

Joan tapped her cheeks. "Boy, take a gander at her. She aged a year in a day."

Queenie squeaked, "She could be a raccoon with those dark circles under her eyes."

Sonia said, "I'm surprised she's working."

Hope tsked, "Poor thing. She must be devastated." Hope stood and pushed in her chair. "I'm gonna invite her to sit with us. No one should be alone at a time like this."

Angela sat between Hope and Joan and across from Queenie, Sonia, and me. Was this the face of mourning or had she been run over by a semi? She blinked her red-rimmed eyes rapidly as though trying to focus. She shredded a napkin to have something to do with her hands. Angela swallowed a glug of coffee and smiled faintly at the faces around the table. "Sorry, I'm afraid I'm not such good company."

Hope soothed, "Angela, we're so sorry for your loss."

Angela's eyes filled, but her laugh was bitter as a lemon rind. "You can't lose what you don't have."

****

I'd procrastinated as long as I could. Fear of loss is a powerful deterrent. Carefree Casuals was a huge account we simply couldn't afford to lose. A lot was riding on this appointment. I put on my big girl panties and called Angela to confirm our meeting. As the phone rang, I made a last-minute plan to stick my neck out and hoped she didn't chop off my head. My stomach clenched as she abruptly answered, "Wellborn, department thirty-six." I made allowances for her grief and went with my overly friendliest salesperson voice reserved for the most difficult buyers. "Hey Angela, it's Holly from Ditzy Swimwear." I chirped with all the enthusiasm of a robin celebrating the first day of spring. "How ya doin' today?"

My reward was a nasty retort. "Listen, I'm jammed, so in ten words or less, what can I do for you?" Yikes. Had Angela Wellborn taken phone etiquette lessons from Sue Ellen Magee? "Calling to cancel? Can't say I'd blame you. Takes a lot of guts to face me on my turf."

If she was this contrary confirming the appointment, the actual meeting should be a real party, if your idea of a fun time was a root canal. This meeting was important, so I swallowed the snappy comeback sitting on the tip of my tongue. "Nope. On the contrary. I'm calling to confirm it."

Angela said, "There's no need for you to come here. We can do it right now. This isn't complicated. You're either gonna work with me or you're outta the store."

Not a chance, sister. You're throwing us out? You're gonna have to do it face to face. "Angela, you're right. We could do it all over the phone, but you are way too important an account to rush through big issues." Should I go with mere contrition or directly to kissing her ass? "We're gonna work with you. As you've pointed out, you're too big an account for us not to. This issue is a small bump in the road. It's a long way until the end of the season, and we've got a lot to discuss regarding business going forward. Our business is too important to plan second hand."

She sighed with resignation. "Fine. It's your funeral."

Not exactly a ringing endorsement, but beggars can't be choosers. Now time to pull the pin off the hand grenade and cross fingers it doesn't explode in my face. "Ah, Angela…"

Her annoyance snapped through the phone like the crack of a whip. "You're my last appointment. Don't even be a minute late. I've no intention of being here all night because of you. You wanna work with me, you better be on time. I'm in meetings all afternoon, with two vendor appointments ahead of yours squeezed in between taking inventory. I have no open time slots, so there's no changing the appointment."

I considered myself lucky. With the way the conversation was going, next she'd tell me to wait in the hall. "Angela…"

"Now what? Make it snappy will ya?" The newly crowned Miss Congeniality of the swimwear industry barked, "Thanks to you, I'm already late for a meeting."

I gritted my teeth. "Angela, Ronnie Schwartzman has disappeared."

"News to me. But wherever he is, he's got an appointment here the same day as yours."

Was she serious? "Angela, I'm pretty sure Ronnie Schwartzman murdered Louis and Bunny."

Her exasperation burned through the phone. "Then the police would have arrested him. Listen, I've gotta go. I don't have time for any more chitchat."

A killer is on the loose, and she's too busy? "Be careful, ok?"

She groaned, "Of what?"

Was she kidding? I didn't want to blow the account before the meeting, so I summoned every drop of patience I still had. "Be careful of Ronnie. He blames you, Louis, and Bunny for all his problems. If he's already punished Bunny and Louis, he'll come after you next."

"If your panties are in a bunch over Ronnie, you can relax. I'm not worried and neither should you." Angela hooted with derision. "Come on, do you see Ronnie Schwartzman as a stone-cold murderer? If you do, get your eyes checked." Angela chortled, "If the self-centered jerk kills anyone, it's by annoying them to death."

From here in the cheap seats, it all pointed to Ronnie. He had to be guilty of something, or why go after me? But listen to Angela, and Ronnie Schwartzman was incapable of killing a cockroach. If Angela was right, I was back at the beginning. If not Ronnie, who? My brain was ready to explode from all the second-guessing.

Angela's raspy voice interrupted my game of mental ping pong. "Oh, don't worry. He'll come after me all right; for his next order." Her laugh was nasty. "And if he ever wants another order, he better live up to the agreement and get his crappy promo off my floor and pronto. Am I scared of Ronnie Schwartzman? Nah. My pencil's too big. Ronnie Schwartzman should be scared of me."

One of these days someone is gonna tell Angela Wellborn exactly where to stick her big pencil.

She said, "Listen, as much fun as this has been, I've gotta go. I'm already ten minutes late for a meeting with Ernie, and he's probably sent out a search party by now." Angela warned, "Don't show up late and don't disappoint me, or I promise you, Ditzy Swimwear is out of the store."

I opened my mouth to say I got the message, but there was no need. Angela wasn't interested in my answer. The whine of the dial tone made it abundantly clear.

Chapter Thirty-Seven

I tried to stay focused on a sales projection, but my mind kept going back to the unsettling conversation with Angela Wellborn. Could she be right? Was Ronnie Schwartzman guilty of nothing more than being a pompous ass? But why did he disappear? Or did he disappear? Who cares if his clothes were out of the showroom? Maybe he and Rhoda kissed and made up? And if Ronnie's boat wasn't still moored at Porto Paloma? What of it? Some boaters change marinas like I change my mind. Maybe the old guy at the Del Rey Yacht Club kicked the bucket and his slip became available? Like the itch I couldn't scratch, the questions chafed at me all day. Bunny Frank didn't truss herself like a Thanksgiving turkey. Queenie and I didn't imagine all the evidence we found. If Ronnie didn't kill Bunny, who did? And was Ronnie responsible for offing Louis? A no-brainer answer had morphed into the question of the century, threatening to drive me insane. I had to get out of the showroom. The walls were beginning to close in on me. Queenie met me at the mart deli. By the time my meal was served, I'd had my fill of second-guessing.

I inhaled my turkey sandwich and Queenie joked, "It's called a lunch hour for a reason. If you're in such a big hurry to get back to work, let Laura pack your sandwich to go."

I smiled sheepishly and related my conversation with Angela.

She asked, "Whaddya wanna do?"

Like she didn't know.

I said, "What's the common denominator to this red-hot mess? Clothing Concepts. Bunny and Louis were both found trussed up and wearing a Gotham swimsuit. The answer has to be somewhere in the showroom. We've gotta go back into Clothing Concepts and figure this thing out. Maybe this time we'll find a smoking gun."

Queenie lectured, "Didn't we agree to give everything to Detective Martinez, and be done?"

I wiggled my digits and grinned. "Nah, I had my fingers crossed. Isn't it possible we missed something?"

She groaned with exasperation. "What's left? Martinez must have gone through those offices with a fine-tooth comb by now."

I gave my pal the big eyes. "Why assume that? Let's not forget how long it took him to pay any attention to us. Ronnie Schwartzman packed his things and ran outta there like his hair was on fire. An innocent man doesn't disappear. He sticks around to clear his name."

Queenie sighed with resignation, but I couldn't shush Nana's voice whispering inside my head. "Things never turn out the way you think they will."

****

Like a couple of second-story guys casing the joint while trying to appear inconspicuous, we walked around the aisle twice before we snuck into the dark Clothing Concepts showroom. Queenie locked the door from the inside, and we went straight to Ronnie's office. We'd done this rodeo so often the place was like a second home.

Queenie arched a brow. "Now what, Nancy Drew?"

I sat behind Ronnie's desk and stared at the blotter. Some great detective I was. I had no idea. The cut-up magazines and the blood-splotched cutting shears were missing. A check of the wastebasket. Empty. "Martinez finally listened and had the evidence taken for testing. Maybe now he has enough to arrest Ronnie." The irony was not lost on me. "But first, he has to find him." I tapped a drumbeat on the desktop. "Or, what if there's another explanation? What if Martinez didn't take me seriously, and all the stuff was still here. What if Ronnie snuck back and took it? Were there two sets of blood-stained shears or one?"

I rooted around inside the desk drawers. The one with the ledger was locked, but the eyeglass case containing the key was gone. Nothing important jumped out at me. The closet behind Ronnie's desk was empty, not even a hanger on the rack.

Queenie closed the bottom drawer of the second cabinet. "This is a big nothing burger. What do you wanna do now?"

"As long as we're here, let's check Louis' office."

The walls had been repainted; the bloody carpeting replaced, but the office was empty, not a stick of furniture. No one would ever guess Louis Chennault had ever occupied the room, let alone died in there.

Queenie gave me the big eyes. "Are we done here, Nancy Drew?"

In so many ways, yes.

As we went our separate ways, Queenie wished me good luck with Angela Wellborn and reminded me we were meeting for dinner at Coast Pizza Parlor at seven-thirty. A victory celebration or a funeral wake? By the time the server sliced the Thai Chicken pizza, would Ditzy Swimwear still be a Carefree Casuals vendor? If Angela threw us out, would I still have a job? Cripes.

****

I stink at this detecting. I questioned a cast of thousands to weed out a killer. And what did I get for my trouble? My car tampered with and my life threatened. Who murdered two prominent industry titans right under my nose? Who is the next victim on their hit list? At the end of the day, the questions buzzed around my brain like a swarm of angry bees, and I still had no answers. I called the one person who might.

The phone rang four times before a familiar voice answered with an official tone. "Cutler, Los Angeles County Coroner's Office. You stab 'em, we slab 'em."

"I'm gonna go out on a limb here and guess the county finally forked out for caller ID?"

My favorite coroner replied, "Nothing gets past you, Nancy Drew."

"And they say government workers have no sense of humor."

Her tone had an impatient inflection. "As much fun as auditioning my comedy routine is, I hate to rush you along, but I've got a patient to get back to. I'm up to my elbows in this guy's brain. I've gotta get back to him before his cerebellum dries out. So, what can I do for you?"

What indeed. I needed another lecture like I needed a hole in my head. I ignored the prickly question. Maybe the truth is overrated? I soldiered on. "I've got questions."

Snip said, "Make it fast."

I got the questions out quickly, before I lost my nerve. "Did you get the tests back yet on the bloody swimsuit and tissues? Was Louis Chennault's mug tested? I noticed brownish liquid at the bottom. Any fingerprints on the cutting shears or the magazines in Ronnie's office?"

Doctor Cutler never missed much. "And you know those items are being tested how?"

I was already in pretty deep; what's one more little lie among friends? "I don't. I suggested Detective Martinez check out the stuff in Ronnie's office, and I was hoping he did."

Her voice dripped with sarcasm. "Uh-huh."

I crossed my fingers and whined, "Honestly, I didn't know."

"Fine, suit yourself. Can you repeat the list? Wait a sec. Hold on and let me get a pencil and some paper. There might be a quiz."

"Funny, like a colonoscopy."

I repeated the questions.

"Anything else, your Royal Majesty?"

I snapped my fingers. Stupid me almost forgot the most important one. "As a matter of fact, there is. I found out most buyers must provide their fingerprints as a hiring requirement. I gave the information to Detective Martinez. Did he manage to pass it along?"

"He did, along with a list of women. We've contacted their HR departments, and the information is starting to come in. No matches yet, but there have only been two to compare. The rest of them should be here today. If we get a hit, it solves the case."

Before my appointment with Angela? A girl could dream. "And the other stuff?"

Snip shot out the answers like a machine gun. "The fingerprints on the magazines, the blood on the swimsuit, the tissues, and the cutting shears are all from the same two men. One is Louis Chennault but no ID on the other man yet. So far, there's no match in the system."

"Gosh if I was a betting girl, I'd go with Ronnie Schwartzman."

Dr. Cutler snarked, "Gee, we might not have figured it out all on our own."

I took a mental bow. "I live to serve."

"Anyway, Miss Wisenheimer, we're on it. We already checked, and Mr. Schwartzman's not in the system. We've contacted the VA. If he was in the military, we can get his records."

And if not? Good luck. Ronnie was still in the wind. Send out the APB. "And the liquid in Louis' mug? Anything besides day-old coffee?"

Doctor Picky Perfectionist replied, "For the record, the liquid was day-old tea, and there was enough digitalis mixed in with it to fell an elephant."

"Isn't digitalis what killed Bunny Frank?"

"It is."

"Are you saying Louis died from digitalis poisoning and not from strangulation?" I closed my eyes. The memory of packing tape tightly wrapped around Louis Chennault's neck made my innards go wonky.

Snip said, "Not conclusive yet. There are still several test results to come back before we can determine if he was trussed pre- or postmortem. I can say if he wasn't already dead when the packing tape was wrapped around his neck, Mr. Chennault was close to it."

Who hated Louis Chennault enough to so viciously murder him? I ran through the names on my mental Rolodex. After Bunny Frank, Martin Decker and Ronnie Schwartzman were the ones who made the hit parade. Martin Decker? Fire Louis? Absolutely. Murder him? As if. Ronnie was still my favorite candidate.

I said, "Bunny and Louis were murdered by the same person? And your needle is still stuck on one person is a she, not a he?"

Snip answered, "Yes, and yes."

My heart sank like a stone skimming across a lake. "I don't get it. With all the evidence I found, how can Ronnie Schwartzman not be the killer?"

"You found some circumstantial evidence to advance your theory to a possible motive. But there's no physical evidence linking Mr. Schwartzman, Mr. Chennault, or any man, to Ms. Frank's murder. The physical evidence is conclusive. Ms. Frank was murdered by a woman. The physical evidence eliminates Mr. Schwartzman and Mr. Chennault."

Undaunted, I sang a different verse of the same song. "Come on, it has to be Ronnie's blood on the shears, the swimsuit, the tissues, and the magazines. I found them in his office. Who else's blood can it possibly be?"

Snip was singing a different tune. "You're convinced Mr. Schwartzman is the killer but try seeing it a different way. Most likely it is Mr. Chennault's blood, but maybe Mr. Schwartzman had a much different reason for being covered in the victim's blood." Her lecturing tone was annoying. "What if Mr. Chennault was still alive? Did you ever consider Mr. Schwartzman tried to save him?"

Ronnie Schwartzman a hero? As if. Ronnie Schwartzman wouldn't give a glass of water to a man dying of thirst unless there was something in it for him. I scoffed, "Try to save him? If Louis was alive, why didn't Ronnie dial nine-one-one?"

Snip cackled like a laying hen. "Considering your, and let us be kind and say, unusual reaction to a death, you should be the last person on the planet to question the way anyone else reacts."

She might be selling, but I wasn't buying. "Innocent men call for help, they don't run away."

Snip burst out laughing. "Oh, come on, give me a break. If you had a rather public fistfight with the decedent and he's found dead in the office next to yours and you were covered with his blood, even if you were innocent, wouldn't you run?"

If you're gonna go and be persnickety, ok yeah. Despite my best efforts, I couldn't come up with a single argument. She had me there.

Chapter Thirty-Eight

Only in Los Angeles does it take over an hour to make a trip, even hitting every red light, that would be a twenty-minute drive anywhere else. I inched along Main Street on my way to Carefree Casuals, and my last conversation with Angela kept replaying like a continuous tape inside my head. Something was off. Don't be late? Don't be early? Don't come at all? The entire conversation was all too weird. Those hairs on the back of my neck stood up again. I could have this all wrong. Joan could be right and Angela murdered Bunny. And Louis Chennault? If Snip was right, now Angela murdered him too? Cripes. Angela had two vendor meetings before mine. One of them was with Ronnie Schwartzman. I assumed if he showed up, he would kill Angela. But now it made no sense. If he killed Bunny and Louis, and so far, gotten away with it, would he be stupid enough to go after Angela now? Ronnie was an arrogant jerk, but he wasn't an idiot. If he was guilty, with his money, the smart move was to fly to Brazil and get lost in the Amazon. If Ronnie was meeting with Angela, there's no way he killed Bunny or Louis. Did he call her for the appointment or was it made at Angela's request? Either way, it didn't matter. If he had an appointment, who says he's gonna show? With all this bouncing around inside my head, it's a wonder I didn't drive myself crazy, or at the least, off the road. Could Snip be right? Maybe Ronnie tried to save Louis. If he did, why did Ronnie run? Six degrees of separation? Because he was guilty or because of how guilty he looked? If not Ronnie, who murdered Louis? An industrial-strength headache pounded like a jackhammer against my skull, and I hadn't even arrived yet at Carefree Casuals. Merde. Since Bunny's murder was the catalyst for everything else, I circled back to who had the most to lose. Ronnie and Louis were still my two favorite candidates, but Ronnie was missing in action, and Louis was dead. After those two, who was left? Angela's name blinked off and on like a klieg light. Cripes. If I was right, I'd be out of my mind to show up for our appointment. But what if I was way off base? So far, I hadn't gotten anything right. Why would I now? My head was spinning. Every time I had the answer, somebody changed the question. Only one way to uncover the truth. I pressed the accelerator and prayed I wasn't driving over a cliff.

****

The receptionist read my name on the sign-in sheet, gave me a badge, and called Angela's assistant. A few minutes later, a frizzy-haired, harassed-looking young woman carrying a clipboard introduced herself and escorted me to the buyers' offices. When we got to Angela's office there was a note taped to the door saying she'd gone out to the loading dock and would be back shortly. The assistant tried Angela's door, but it was locked. Megan said, "I'm surprised she's not back. She's been gone quite a while. I've been with the display team for most of the afternoon. She must have put the note on her door while I was with them." Megan's pride shone in her eyes. "You'd love the cute advertising display Angela and I designed. Two young moms with their kids all wearing swimsuits sitting in a sandbox building a castle. The prototype arrived today. I had the display team leave it on the loading dock for Angela. All I need is Angela's approval and I can order duplicates for the stores. Be sure Angela shows it to you. We used two Ditzy Swimwear suits in your cool Paradise print for the young moms." Megan tapped her fingertip to a calendar attached to the clipboard. "Those styles will be the first ones on the advertising display when our spring break ads hit." Megan's eyes lit. "Your sales should spike quite a bit."

The display sounded terrific. The question was, would any Ditzy Swimwear suits still be in stock to display by the time the ad broke?

Megan opened the door to a small office next to Angela's. She put the clipboard on the desk and took her purse out of the bottom drawer. "Listen, I'm sorry, but I've gotta go. I'm already late picking up my kid. Daycare charges a dollar for every minute you're late, no excuses and no exceptions." She smiled. "Before I have to sell my firstborn to pay them, I've gotta get outta here. Hopefully, Angela won't be too long." She jiggled Angela's door handle again and sighed. "I hate leaving you out in the hall. Why don't you wait in my office?"

I waved her off. "Nah, don't worry." I wiggled my brows and laughed. "Angela wants something from me. She won't be too long."

Megan locked her office door and left me standing in the hall. I opened my briefcase and paged through the Carefree Casuals file. Crap. Good thing I checked. Before I left for the appointment, I'd taken out a spreadsheet for a last-minute check on the numbers.

After Angela's lecture on promptness, I rushed out of the office to be on time. Most likely the spreadsheet was sitting on my desk. Thank God for cell phones. I'd call Hope and ask her to fax it to Angela's office.

I put the file on the floor and rooted through my purse. No phone. Double crap. I ran my fingers inside my briefcase. I stabbed my pinky on a paperclip, but no phone. I emptied everything on the floor, but no luck. I crammed the stuff back into my briefcase and walked around the buyer's cube, but all the offices were locked. I went back to reception, but the desk was unmanned. I bent over the phone bank and fumed. Leave it to a retailer to put a lock on the phones. No guest phone, no paging phone, not even a tin can on a string. Was there not a single payphone left in the whole country? I mentally retraced my steps. I had the cell when I left the office. It had to be in the car, but I couldn't go out to check. With no one in reception, there was no way to get back into the building.

If Angela was back in her office and I wasn't there, she'd be furious. This meeting had already become a disaster before it even began. I speed-walked back to the buyer's cube. Good news, bad news. The note was still taped on Angela's door.

I passed a sign pointing to the loading dock on the way back to the buyer's cube. There was nothing left to do but go to the loading dock. If Angela wasn't still there, I'd missed her and blown the meeting. Visions of Ditzy Swimwear being thrown out of the store and my career going out with it were all I could see.

Chapter Thirty-Nine

The pathway to the loading dock was dark as a cave. With only dim emergency floor lights to illuminate it, the direction signs were almost impossible to read. I lurched along the path like I was playing blind man's bluff. I squinted in the distance. Faintly lighter. The pathway didn't lead anywhere else. Had to be the loading dock.

What would I find when I got there? An ocean of Gotham swimsuits, no doubt. Would Ronnie's corpse be draped across them? Had I sealed Ronnie's fate with my conversation with Angela? Guilt gnawed at my heart. I had to talk to Detective Martinez. And say what? That I couldn't decide whether Angela or Ronnie had murdered Bunny and Louis? Ought to go over like a fart in church. I shook off the idea.

What if I actually had any valuable information? Unless telepathy or tea leaves work, I was out of luck. I had another option. I could always leave. Oh, yeah; another brilliant idea. I could also have it all wrong and where would I be? After not showing up for this meeting, in the unemployment line. Cripes. The loading dock was lit, so Angela must still be there. I squared my shoulders and kept going.

I almost peed myself as icy fingers brushed across my back. Security guard? Megan? Angela? Ronnie Schwartzman? Bunny's ghost? Louis' spirit? Jack the Ripper? I clenched my fingers into tight fists, prepared to take on my attacker. I turned and collapsed against the wall. Should I laugh or cry? I'd bumped into one of the mannequins lined up like sentries on the opposite side of the path. I whispered my apologies to the dummy and kept walking toward the light.

As though the light ahead shined a beam of illumination, it all fell into place. My synapses snapped like a live wire and, in a moment of clarity, I realized I'd been wrong all along. How could I be so blind with everything right in front of me all the time? The motive was revenge, but not over getting stuck with a bunch of unsold bikinis. The motive was revenge over love and betrayal.

Angela was head over heels in love with Louis. She murders Bunny, and it's a neat one-two punch. Angela punishes Bunny for her promo problems and eliminates her as a rival for Louis at the same time. But when Louis' affair with Shannon Decker came out, Angela realized Louis was only using her to camouflage his affair with the boss' wife. Angela's response to our condolences hit me like a ton of bricks. You can't lose what you don't have.

Bunny and Louis died from digitalis poisoning. What did Snip say the stuff was made from? I racked my brain. A byproduct of Foxglove. I'm such an idiot. Mental head slap. Angela is a master gardener. Foxglove is a common garden plant. Angela probably grows it by the acre. She could have ground the leaves the way Snip described and poisoned Bunny and Louis. Merde.

Both of them were found with a Gotham swimsuit attached to their bodies. No problem getting her hands on them; Angela probably had a lifetime supply. Same with the packing tape. She had plenty of motive and means. Did she have the opportunity?

Carefree Casuals was one of Bunny's major accounts. Angela could come up with a pretext to meet with Bunny, and Bunny wouldn't suspect a thing. Go someplace neutral like A Jolt of Java, sprinkle Foxglove powder into Bunny's drink, get her into the parking garage, and finish her off? Pretty plausible.

Maybe Angela helped Louis pack and then killed him? Or she killed him first and packed his stuff afterward to throw the cops off? Could have happened either way. Holy guacamole.

And then there's me. Someone with mechanical expertise had messed with my car. Either I'd angered the killer, or I was close to cracking the case. Who tried to scare me out of sniffing around? Blinking signs pointed to Ronnie and Louis. The first one didn't know the difference between a lug nut from a coconut, and the second one did, but he was in jail when the car was tampered with.

The distributor cap and the icepick were hidden in Ronnie's golf bag, but who's to say Ronnie put them there? If someone wanted to frame him, they could have been planted. Somebody was working overtime to point the finger at Ronnie and used me to help them do it. With Louis gone, who was left? No matter which way the deck was shuffled, the person dealing the cards in this deadly game of chance didn't change. Angela Wellborn. The question is why? Certainly not over a canceled order. Louis Chennault. Angela must blame me for Louis' arrest. With convoluted logic, she could also blame me for his murder. Why push to cancel our meeting? Wouldn't she want to keep it to finish me off?

Or maybe I had this wrong too? Was I giving myself too much credit? Cripes. This must be what Peso feels like when he's chasing his tail.

If I was right, going into the loading dock wasn't exactly a brain surgeon move. I did a one-eighty back to the lobby, but there was still no one around. What store doesn't have a security guard? Did Angela knock him off too?

I had to get my phone. An alarm panel blinked at the main entrance. What if I opened the door and the alarm went off? It might not be such a bad thing. Gets the cops here fast and maybe nobody gets hurt. I pulled on the handle. Remarkably, the door opened, and no alarms sounded. Curious. Did somebody, like the killer, disarm it, or was it a silent alarm? One could hope for door number two. I'd find out soon enough.

I wedged my briefcase between the door and the doorjamb and willed the door to stay open. I recognized Ronnie Schwartzman's Mercedes 500 with its vanity plate GOTH BIK. Aside from the mustang, the only other car in the lot had to be Angela's sedan.

I keyed the mustang and slid into the driver's seat. The phone was wedged between the passenger seat and the center console. I shoved my hand into the crevice and stretched my fingers as far as they'd go. I could touch the top of the phone, but I was at an odd angle and couldn't get my hand in far enough to grab it. I got out of the car and leaned in, ass in the air, so I could see between the seat and the console. I took the hairbrush out of my purse and used it to move the phone close enough to get my fingers around it. I pushed in against the side of the seat for traction and after three tries, I pulled the phone free.

I hit the start button and prayed the phone wasn't dead. My charger was in my briefcase, but I didn't have time to search for an electrical outlet to recharge it. Hallelujah. I still had some juice; two bars ought to be plenty. I dialed Detective Martinez, but he didn't answer. I left him a message and hoped I didn't sound too hysterical. With any luck, he checked his voicemail more often than I check mine. I tried Snip at the morgue and on her cell phone, but all I got was voicemail. Friday night. The world was out having a good time while I'm trying to save Ronnie Schwartzman's life. Cripes.

I locked the car and went back to the store entrance. The door was still wedged open. I grabbed my briefcase and went inside. Now, what? The logical answer? Sit in the reception, pray Martinez and Snip check their messages, and wait for the cavalry to ride in. Was Ronnie already dead? Then it wouldn't matter how long the cavalry took. And if he was still alive? I couldn't wait for help to arrive. I threw logic out the window and went back to the loading dock.

Chapter Forty

When I got close enough to the entrance to see, there was Angela, surrounded by racks and racks of Gotham swimwear. Boy, the promo program had been a nuclear bomb.

Angela was talking and Ronnie Schwartzman was answering. That they were having a conversation is a good thing, right? At least nobody was dead…yet. Had I overreacted and they were working things out? If so, Angela had no reason to cancel my orders. Could this hot mess have a happy ending after all? I leaned in closer to find out. Angela's husky voice carried. She wasn't in fear for her life; she was reading Ronnie the riot act.

I was still too far away from the details. All I made out were loud voices and garbled words. I inched forward. I didn't want to miss Ronnie Schwartzman finally get the comeuppance he deserved. When I got to the loading dock entrance, I stopped short and shoved my fist in my mouth to stifle a scream. Angela Wellborn was holding a gun on Ronnie Schwartzman. Ronnie didn't sound too arrogant right then as he pleaded for his life.

****

The wounds from Ronnie's slugfest with Louis were healing. Ronnie's nose was splinted straight, and his missing teeth had been replaced. His shiner had lost its green and purple tinge, and his eyelid fluttered open with the swelling gone. His eye was still ringed by a black circle. His face resembled Frankenstein less and more like a raccoon who'd duked it out with a possum and lost the first round. Would Ronnie live long enough to fully recover? Not if Angela Wellborn had her way.

Ronnie's plea gurgled from the back of his throat and came out like a strangled sob. "Angela, why are you doing this to me?"

Angela waved the pistol at the racks of Gotham swimsuits and snorted like a razorback. "Are you kidding? You ruined my career with your fabulous promo program."

His voice was tinny as he whined, "Angela, we can work this out." Ronnie brushed his bandaged hand across the swimsuits. "I already agreed to take all the suits back." Ronnie sweetened the deal. "I'll even give you the same terms on all your future orders. You don't need to do this."

Angela's laugh was bitter as burnt toast. "Too little, too late. You got me fired."

Ronnie uttered the same question out loud I muttered under my breath. "When were you fired?"

If I had a brain, I would have run for my life. Instead, I was rooted to the spot, intent on listening to Angela spit out the words like a piece of rotten fruit. "The morning before lowlife Bunny Frank got what she deserved. Ernie called me into his office and gave me a choice of resigning or being fired."

Ronnie's jaw dropped at the same time as mine.

Angela snickered, "Pretty shocked huh?"

Ronnie and I wagged our heads like a couple of agreeable Airedales.

"Yeah," Angela spat. "Get in line and take a number. Pretty ironic when you consider I had nothing to do with writing the promo order."

Who did?

As though she heard me, Angela said, "Ernie and Bunny wrote it while I was in Mexico on vacation." Angela's smile was nasty. "Bunny probably gave ole Ernie one heck of a good time to get the huge order he wrote. Leave it to a man to think with the wrong head."

Sonia Wilson's comment flitted through my memory. Gack.

Angela jabbed the pistol out like she was fencing. "And yet who does he blame when the stuff doesn't sell?" Angela waved the gun at Ronnie's head. "Who does he blame when the vendor won't live up to the deal?"

Ronnie had the grace to blush.

Angela screeched, "Me!" Angela cackled, "Then the senile old fool ordered me into the market to cancel off styles we're selling like hotcakes." Angela viciously raked the gun across one of the racks. "When none of my vendors accepted the cancellations, the moron fired me." Angela held up her free hand and corrected herself. "No, he magnanimously let me resign." Angela arced the gun in the air like a majorette twirling a baton. "And for all my years of loyalty and devotion, for all my hard work, I got a token to avoid the lawsuit package so puny it won't even buy me a decent gardening hoe." She curled her upper lip. "He made me finish inventory before he'd authorize my severance. Today's my last day, and you're all gonna pay." Angela's eyes blazed wild. "I called Bunny to meet me at A Jolt of Java in the mart. I threw the party, so I sprang for the drinks." Angela's smile was pure evil. "When the barista handed me the two coffees, I added my special treat to Bunny's." Angela glanced at a wall clock and cringed. "We finished our coffee when A Jolt of Java was closing and the mart was deserted. Bunny wouldn't let me wait in the dark for the minibus. She insisted on driving me back to the store. By the time we got into the parking garage, Bunny was sick as a dog. We hadn't even made it to her car when she collapsed." Angela's hollow smile was as haunting as a ghost story. "Bunny was gasping for air and too weak to fight. I dragged her into the elevator. When the door closed, I hit the stop button and propped her against the back of the car." Angela's eyes fluttered dreamily. "As she lay dying, she held her arms out and begged me for help. I whispered in her ear I'd see her in hell first. She choked out why? She asked, was it the promo? But I laughed in her face; an eye for an eye. She destroyed Louis' life, so I destroyed hers." Angela slapped her knee. "Wasn't the bikini in her mouth a nice touch?" Angela waggled her brows. "Pretty smart, huh? Pointed things right to you." Angela smacked a rack with the gun barrel and hooted like an owl. "I certainly had enough of them to choose from." Angela sighed. "And there was Louis." Angela's eyes filled. "I gave him my heart, and he broke it. I loved him more than life itself. I killed for him. What more did he want?" Angela choked. "I sold my soul for Louis Chennault. Why wasn't it enough?" Ronnie jumped out of the way when Angela viciously kicked a rolling rack at him. "I was nothing more to Louis than a useful tool to hide his affair with a married tramp." Angela's macabre smile was the spitting image of the Grim Reaper. "He betrayed my trust. He deserved to die." Angela made a pouring gesture like the barrel of the gun was a coffee pot. "We were half-way finished packing all his crap and took a coffee break. Like Manners the Butler he told me he'd be right back with it; there was a fresh pot brewing in the kitchen." Angela's cackle cut through the air like the blade of a knife. "While he was gone, I added a little something special to his mug of tea. By the time the break was over, Louis Chennault was on the way to his special place in hell."

Yikes. Payback is nasty. Angela waved the gun at Ronnie. "Too bad you weren't in your office. After I took care of Louis, you were gonna be next." Angela's eyes glittered. "But here you are now. Once I finish you off, the scales will be even." Angela rolled her eyes. "How could the dumb cop not arrest you? The only thing I didn't do is shine a blinking light. I planted evidence on your desk, in your wastebasket, and in your golf bag, I framed you for accidents. I even took the same sample out of your line I shoved in Bunny's mouth." The clock ticked away another hour and Angela sighed. "Some detective. A clueless idiot who should be writing parking tickets."

Way to go, Nancy Drew. Better keep your day job. Was it possible to get this one any more wrong?

She waved the gun at Ronnie. "The cop didn't do his job, so I have to do it for him."

Keep her talking you moron, I silently urged.

Ronnie's face shone wet with perspiration. "Angela, I don't own the company. I'm a worker bee. Martin's the one who sets company policies; not me." He whined, "I had no choice but to follow his rules."

Nana's voice whispered be careful what you wish for.

Angela snorted like a hog in heat. "Oh, isn't this rich. Five minutes ago, you had the authority to give me all my orders on wheels, and now you're a powerless worker bee? Nice try, Mr. Manufacturer, but no dice. The knife doesn't slice both ways." Angela growled, "You could have lived up to the deal if you'd wanted to, but you're a pig." Angela grinned a toothy smile. "You know what they say doncha? Pigs get slaughtered. And now you will too."

Angela trained the gun at his chest, and Ronnie sobbed, "Angela, please. I've got a wife and kids."

Angela laughed like a loon. "Oh my God, you are hilarious. Now the little wife and kiddies are a worry? You weren't too worried about them while you screwed Bunny Frank's brains out." Angela snickered at Ronnie's stunned expression. "Don't be too shocked. Bunny bragged she was messing around with you for fun and profit." Angela sneered, "Doncha get it, Ronnie? Bunny weaponized you. She used you to destroy Louis Chennault. There was nothing sacred to Bunny Frank, least of all screwing around with an arrogant, clueless jerk like you." Angela waved the gun like she was leading an orchestra. "We've wasted enough time. Enjoy the trip, Ronnie. Your place in hell is waiting for you."

Chapter Forty-One

Angela leveled the gun at Ronnie's heart. Why isn't there ever a cop around when you need one? What do they say? Ask and ye shall receive? The question was answered when my cell phone rang. BRRRRNG, BRRRRNG! Loudly. Mental head slap. Now's a good time to remember the vibrate function. Oops. My bad.

Angela and Ronnie automatically patted their pockets. While they were busy figuring out which one of their phones were ringing, I made a run for it. As I backed away, the heel of my shoe got caught on a wheel of one of the rolling racks. I tripped and fell unceremoniously on my ass.

Angela pivoted sideways at the clash of steel and flesh. The sight of me sprawled out on the floor sent her into hysterics. "If it isn't little Miss Persistent." My blood ran cold when she mused, "You had a helluva good run, but I guess your luck finally ran out." Angela stared at the clock again and groused, "I can't believe you hung around waiting for me. Yet here you are still mucking things up." Angela hooted, "Bet this is one appointment you wish you hadn't kept."

No kidding.

Angela grabbed the cell phone out of my hand when it rang again. She threw it on the ground and stomped it into a hundred pieces. Does the warranty cover this? Angela waved the gun in Ronnie's direction. "Get over there next to the captain of industry and let's get this thing done."

I glared at imbecile Ronnie. Why didn't he rush her when he had the chance? Didn't he get the bulletin? God helps those who help themselves. Ronnie might be ready to die, but I wasn't. I slid my eyes to the right. A rack loaded with swimsuits was close enough to grab. I edged step by tiny step closer to the rack. I hooked my arm around the backs of the swimsuits for leverage. I prayed the plastic hangers didn't squeak on the metal bar as I pushed the swimsuits to the left. I held my breath. The swimsuits jostled when their weight shifted. Did Angela notice? She didn't shoot me; so far so good.

With no time to develop an actual game plan, I punted. Words bypassed my brain and jumped out of my mouth all on their own. My heart pounded like a bass drum, but my voice was amazingly calm. "Angela, please, you're better than this. Tell the cops you were caught in a situation you had no control over. Bunny got you into a mess and Louis left you hung out to dry. At least a sharp lawyer will get you the help you need." I flicked a wrist at Ronnie. "But kill both of us? The cops aren't braindead. They'll figure it out. And all bets will be off. Don't make it worse for yourself. You're a smart woman. Angela, I am talking to you as a friend. Please don't do this."

Any chance I had of talking my way out of this catastrophe was lost as Angela dismissed me with a sweep of the gun. "My life is ruined, and all of you are gonna pay." Her eyes were hard as granite. "Your meddling got Louis arrested. Your interference got him killed. And if you didn't keep sticking your nose where it didn't belong, you wouldn't have gotten involved in all this. But no, you couldn't let it go. I warned you over and over, but you didn't pay any attention." She lectured, "You should have listened, you should have taken the hint, but you didn't, and this is where it got you. Now you're another loose end I've gotta tie up along with him."

The metallic taste of fear bit my tongue, and the words she meant to comfort terrified me more.

"Don't worry," she soothed. "It'll be fast; you won't suffer. My daddy was a hunter. I've been around guns all my life. I'm a crack shot. You'll hardly feel a thing." Angela aimed the gun at the rack standing next to her and shot a hole through the center of the swimsuits hanging on the bar. She giggled at her handiwork. "Now they're a perfect fit."

Angela pointed the gun back at us, and selfishly I hoped this was one-time ladies didn't go first. As Angela cocked the hammer, an overhead fluorescent light fixture made a popping noise. A lightbulb blew out, and the other lights flickered. Angela instinctively turned toward the sound. The time was now or never. I shoved the packed rolling rack into Angela's midsection with everything I had. The rack made a satisfyingly loud whoomph as it hit her in the breadbasket. All the air whooshed out of her lungs, and she deflated like a leaky balloon. The momentum of the rack sent her pinwheeling backward. Angela got a shot off before she landed, and Ronnie screamed like a little girl. Angela went down with all the grace of a sack of potatoes. The irony was not lost on me; she was buried beneath a mountain of Gotham swimsuits.

Angela dropped the gun as she fell backward. Remarkably it didn't go off when it hit the ground and bounced in front of Ronnie. I pointed at the pistol and yelled, "Get the gun and cover her!" I took a step toward the dark hallway. "I'll go back to the lobby and find help. There's gotta be a security guard around here somewhere."

Ronnie picked up the gun and aimed it at me. "Don't bother. We're not gonna need any help from a Renta-cop. I've got the situation under control."

Huh?

Ronnie's right thigh was gushing blood like a geyser. Had he lost his mind? Of course we needed help. The cops had to arrest Angela, and if the paramedics didn't get here pretty fast, Ronnie would bleed to death.

Ronnie swayed as he pressed his right hand over the wound trying to stem the bleeding. He held the gun in his left hand and still had it aimed at me.

I pointed to his hemorrhaging thigh. "Listen to me. If you don't let me go for help, you're gonna bleed to death, Ronnie." Annoyance crept into my voice. "For crying out loud, you're holding the gun on the wrong person." I pointed to the pile of swimsuits with Angela lying underneath. "Don't cover me, cover her."

Ronnie growled, "Don't tell me what to do. I'm not an idiot."

Could have fooled me.

Ronnie waved the gun in Angela's direction. "Get over by her."

My brain and my feet weren't talking to one another. My tootsies were cemented to the ground.

Ronnie screamed, "Do it now!" And he was the slow-witted one? He was a regular Einstein compared to me. When the proverbial light bulb clicked on, it almost blinded me. Ding, ding it finally hit me. Ronnie Schwartzman was going to kill me. The realization I was going to die took my breath away. If I didn't get a hold of myself, I'd never make it out of this mess alive. "Ronnie, stop before you do something you can't undo."

Ronnie snickered. "It's a little late. The ship has already sailed." He pointed the gun at Angela. "She was gonna kill me. This is self-defense."

"Why kill her? She's the murderer, not you. Hold the gun on her. Let me go for help. The cops arrive, they arrest her, and she goes to prison for the rest of her life."

Ronnie took his palm off his thigh to wipe it on his shirt and a gush of blood squirted out like a wildcatter's oil derrick. At the rate Ronnie was losing blood, Angela's shot must have hit an artery. He covered the wound with his palm and pressed, but he couldn't staunch the flow of blood. Time wasn't on his side. He was sinking faster than a torpedoed battleship. He swayed like a palm tree during a hurricane but managed to stay on his feet.

Cripes, I couldn't catch a break.

I reasoned, "Don't do anything stupid. Stop before it's too late."

Ronnie growled like a cornered dog. "Shut up and get next to her."

I edged toward Angela to placate him. I eyed the racks full of swimsuits, but they were too far away. Besides, there was no element of surprise. I searched desperately for a weapon, but nothing jumped out. Keep him talking, I told myself. "Why are you doing this? You've got the life we all envy. Great job, power, and money. I don't get it. Why do you want to throw it all away?"

"Too late. There's nothing to throw away. It's already gone."

I couldn't believe my ears. "What?"

Ronnie spat, "Martin fired me. I agreed to meet with Angela to try to change Martin's mind. Now it doesn't matter. Once word gets out I've been canned, I'm finished in the industry."

"Why? Clothing Concepts isn't the only game in town. You're a big deal in the industry. There are lots of other companies who would do anything to get you on their team. Don't throw your life away."

"You," Ronnie snarled, "are the most annoying bitch in the business."

And all this time the smart money bet the honor went to Sue Ellen Magee.

He said, "Bunny's stunt created a huge enough problem, but she's not the one who got me fired. Here I'm trying to do the right thing for my company and what do I get? I get canned. And who can I thank?" Ronnie pointed to the two size- ten shoes sticking out from under the pile of swimsuits. "Her." Ronnie's laugh was evil. "And I'm gonna repay her with exactly what she deserves."

Ronnie mused to himself, "I should have taken care of you when I had the chance." He smirked. "Who says there are no second chances? There would have been a problem explaining things to the cops before." He grinned. "But now it's all gonna work out fine and dandy, thanks to you."

I took a mental bow. I live to serve.

Ronnie's smile was wicked. "When the cops arrive, I'll tell them the truth. I was lured over here to work out the problem with the promos. But when I got to the loading dock like she instructed me to, Angela pulled out a gun." Ronnie licked his chops. "She was furious when you showed up and disrupted her plans for me. She threatened to shoot you first. I'm a good guy and tried to save you. I rushed her. Angela and I fought. During the struggle, the gun went off. She was aiming for me but I batted the gun barrel away. Regrettably, the gun pointed at you, and she shot you dead." Ronnie took his right hand off his thigh, and a fountain of blood squirted into the air. "We wrestled, she shot me in the thigh, and I wrenched the gun away from her. She was crazed, a maniac. She grabbed for the gun, and I had to shoot her in self-defense."

I hated the outcome, but the story was a plausible one. Cripes.

Ronnie waved the gun at me. "I warned you to mind your own business. Now you're gonna be sorry you didn't."

Ok, I'm a touch nosy, but now you're gonna shoot me? Seriously?

As though he read my mind, he said, "I've got no choice. You know too much."

I promise to keep my yip shut.

"Ok, enough talk." He swept the gun to Angela. "Let's get this show on the road."

Dozens of swimsuits were strewn all over the floor when Angela sat up. Her mocking laughter echoed through the loading dock like a Jack in the box on crack. "What a fabulous alibi." She gave him a round of applause and snorted her ridicule. “You’d probably get away with it. Too bad you don’t have the guts to do it.”

Ronnie’s grin was as wide as a Cheshire Cat’s. “Gee, Angela, this is where you’re dead wrong.” Ronnie dried his bloody hand on his pants, aimed the gun barrel at Angela’s head, and fired a single shot. Angela’s skull exploded as the bullet shattered the center of her forehead. As her body fell back into the pile of swimsuits, her lips were forever frozen in the shape of a surprised O.

No kidding. I was right there with her. Ronnie’s laugh chilled my blood to ice. He had the gun sighted at the same spot on my forehead. Ronnie’s complexion was gray as wet cement, and his eyes drooped at half-mast. He’d lost an awful lot of blood. A light breeze could probably tip him over. Could I? I estimated my chances. As if. Even with him wounded, the possibilities of me taking a guy so much taller and heavier were slimsky to nonesky. But with no weapon, tackling him was the only option.

I planted my feet and steeled myself for combat, but Ronnie never gave me the opportunity to find out. He lurched a half dozen steps until he was standing directly in front of me. Rivulets of perspiration poured down his face. He swiped at the sweat running into his eyes with the heel of a bloody hand. The salty sweat mixed with the blood. It had to sting, but did it impair his vision? If not, his shot better be off-kilter or I’m as dead as Angela. He lifted the gun and aimed. I closed my eyes and whispered a prayer.

One beat, a second, and a third. He didn’t fire. Not to look a gift horse in the mouth; but why didn’t he shoot? Had he discovered his conscience and chose to spare me? As if. I cracked open an eye. The blood on his hands had transferred onto the trigger. He tried to pull it back, but his index finger kept slipping off.

I swiveled my head in search of anything to stop him with. The advertising display Megan had described stood a few feet away. For once, being a shorty worked in my favor. I was already low to the ground. Before Ronnie could react, I dove to the floor. I tucked my knees into my abdomen and rolled like a beachball. I grabbed two fists of sand from the sandbox. I powered up with my knees and threw the sand in Ronnie's eyes.

He screamed and dropped the gun. He scrubbed at his eyes with his bloody fists, embedding the sand even deeper. He pinwheeled his arms and staggered around like a blind man trying to dance. I aimed like a game-winning field goal was at stake and landed my kick in the center of his bloody wound. Ronnie screeched like a banshee and fell in a heap on top of a pile of swimsuits.

I grabbed the pistol off the floor, wiped Ronnie's blood off the gun with the tail of my shirt, and hoped I wouldn't shoot myself instead of him. I mentally patted myself on the back. I managed to hold the gun by the grip, not by the barrel, and aimed the business end of the pistol at Ronnie's head. The gun weighed a ton. I needed both hands to keep it level. Think holding a cannon steady with your fingertips.

Time wasn't my friend. Ronnie was out cold but not for long. I searched the room for something to restrain him with. A huge dispenser of shipping tape sat on a packing table. Terrific. Hold the gun on Ronnie and try tying him with one hand? Not possible. Put the gun on the table and use two hands? Not a chance. My mother didn't raise stupid children.

It didn't take long for my sweaty hands to ache and my fingers to cramp like an arthritic old lady's. My leaden arms grew number by the minute. Soon they'd be limp as overcooked noodles. Help better arrive before my arms gave out along with my bravado.

Where were the good guys when you need them?

Finally, a male voice shouted, "Freeze!"

No problemo. I stood still as a statue.

Did the security guard finally come on duty? Nope, I recognized the voice. Detective Martinez. The cavalry finally arrived. Hallelujah.

I called out, "Hey, Martinez. It's me, Holly Schlivnik. Detective, I'm back here on the loading dock. I need help. Please hurry."

Martinez stopped at the entrance to the loading dock and barked an order that was music to my ears. "Drop your weapons!"

Gladly, detective. I set the gun on the floor and stepped on the grip. I raised my hands to the sky and cried out, "Don't shoot!" as Martinez and an army of gun-toting LAPD uniforms stormed the loading dock.

Then I fainted.

Epilogue

Sophie Cutler and I met for dinner at The Gallery on Main Street, the oldest restaurant and bar in Santa Monica. Dinner was my treat to celebrate my remarkably surprising survival.

Snip indelicately snorted her wine spritzer out through her nose as I recounted the string of voicemails I received from Queenie that fateful Friday night. "When I was twenty minutes late, Queenie called and asked what was taking so long? She read me the daily specials and offered to order one for me. Ten minutes later her next message wasn't nearly as nice. After asking where the hell was I already, she said she was starving." I wagged an index finger. "No, wait. Let me get it right. Oh yeah, now I remember. She was wasting away to nothing and could I please move my ass a little faster or she'd start eating without me. The next one is my personal favorite." I slapped the table and hooted, "She wanted to know if Angela Wellborn had stabbed me with her big pencil. Her last one was she asked if I had killed Angela, and was I almost finished burying the body?"

Six degrees of separation.

Snip grinned. "There had to be a problem. You're never late when Thai chicken pizza is involved."

I said, "My special relationship with Thai Chicken pizza is no state secret, so what took Queenie so long to realize something was wrong?"

Snip asked, "Isn't your pet peeve how often buyers keep vendors waiting?"

Often? Try most of the time. No one's time is valuable but theirs.

Snip dipped a shoulder. "Your friend assumed Ms. Wellborn kept you waiting and your meeting ran late." Snip cuffed my shoulder and smiled kindly. "You're not the best at checking messages, but you don't ignore that many. Your friend called Ms. Wellborn's office. When Ms. Wellborn didn't answer or return the message, your friend realized something was wrong."

I joked, "Yeah, something was wrong. My pal was facing imminent starvation."

Snip raised her eyebrows to her hairline. "Your friend gave the detective quite an earful. She was furious how long he took to call her back." Snip laughed. "After all, she only left a half-dozen messages."

I clucked my tongue. "Patience is not exactly one of Queenie's strong suits." Thank God.

Snip said, "Martinez freaked out when she told him you were meeting with Angela Wellborn at her office."

I gave her the big eyes. "Why? After the way he'd brushed us off, I'm surprised he didn't tell her I was stuck in traffic and to chill out."

Snip held her index finger in the air. "I can help you out there. I received Ms. Wellborn's fingerprints the same time you were arriving at her office. They were a match to those found at the Frank crime scene. Martinez got a search warrant for Ms. Wellborn's home. He was there when your friend was trying to call him. You were right, Ms. Wellborn was a master gardener. There was an enormous garden in the back of her house. In the center was a large bed of Foxglove."

The fingers of regret gripped my insides and twisted them around. If I remembered Angela was a master gardener sooner, I'd have saved us all a lot of trouble. Cripes. "Angela was acting pretty weird when I confirmed our appointment. She discouraged me from coming to the office. Suggested we should work out what we had to over the phone. When I insisted on keeping the appointment, she made it clear she had no earlier time slots available. And she warned me not to be late because she wouldn't wait around for me all night." I wrinkled my forehead. "Weird, huh?"

Snip shook her head no. "She had a good reason. Ms. Wellborn couldn't have you arrive early and interrupt her killing Mr. Schwartzman. She had no intention of being there for your appointment. She planned to lure Mr. Schwartzman to her office, kill him, and get far away fast. Ms. Wellborn had an exit plan, and you insisting on keeping your appointment loused it up big time."

I sighed. "Beyond my wildest dreams."

Snip said, "Detective Martinez found two packed suitcases in the trunk of Ms. Wellborn's car. Along with her passport, there were ten thousand dollars in cash and a one-way ticket for a flight to Barcelona hidden under the spare tire."

I slapped my cheek. "Ah. No wonder she kept checking the time." I did the mental around the world tour and frowned. "Barcelona? Odd she picked a high-profile place like Spain. Why not one of those obscure little countries in the middle of nowhere that doesn't have an extradition agreement with the United States?"

Snip quirked a smile. "Actually, she did. She wasn't planning on staying in Barcelona, she was only passing through. She had a map of Andorra and a voucher for a one-way bus ticket in her passport folder. It's a three-hour bus ride from Barcelona to Andorra la Vella."

I was pretty good at geography but this was one country I wasn't familiar with. "Andorra? Where is it?"

Snip re-arranged her silverware and fashioned it into a map. "None of us had any idea. Martinez had to Google it." She pointed to a spot between a butter knife and a teaspoon. "It's a tiny country sandwiched between France and Spain in the eastern part of the Pyrenees mountains. It's known for great skiing and has no extradition agreement with this country."

I snickered. "How did she pick it? Close her eyes and throw a dart at a map of the world?"

Snip laughed out loud. "Nah. Martinez dug around the Wellborn family tree and discovered Ms. Wellborn's mother's side was originally from there. Ms. Wellborn was fluent in both Spanish and Catalan, the language spoken in Andorra. The Catalan connection helped Detective Martinez figure out Ms. Wellborn was who tried to frame Ms. Wilson."

I blinked my confusion. "How?"

Snip held her cell phone to her ear. "Ms. Wellborn called in the anonymous tip to the police regarding Ms. Wilson's altercation with Ms. Frank. It took time for Martinez to put it together because Ms. Wellborn didn't use her own phone. She used her mother's cell. Ms. Wellborn's mother goes by her maiden name, not her husband's. Her maiden name is Bernat, a common

Catalan surname. Bernat is the name tied to the cell phone carrier her mother used."

I snapped my fingers. "Angela and I walked into A Jolt of Java together the morning Sonia and Bunny argued. Angela's table was next to Bunny's. She couldn't miss Sonia pour the latte over Bunny's head and threaten Bunny."

Snip finished the story. "But when Ms. Wilson was released from custody, Ms. Wellborn lost her perfect patsy. Ms. Wellborn changed tactics and tried framing Mr. Schwartzman. She had no way of knowing science had eliminated any men as suspects in Ms. Frank's murder."

I sighed. "Better keep my day job. I suck at detecting. Turns out Martinez was right all along, and I was way off base."

Snip patted me on the shoulder. "Don't be so hard on yourself. If you didn't tip off Martinez on the retailer fingerprint requirements for employment, Ms. Wellborn would probably have gotten away with it."

I shook my head no. "I can't take credit for the tip. I was only the messenger. Ironically, Sonia Wilson made it possible for Martinez to break the case. So, Angela took the swimsuit out of Ronnie's sample line? And Angela planted the bloody shears, the icepick, the distributor cap, and the packing tape in Ronnie's golf bag?"

Snip grinned. "You betcha. When the Coast Guard recovered Mr. Schwartzman's boat, the evidence you photographed was still on the vessel." Snip wiggled her fingers. "We ran everything through the lab, and Ms. Wellborn's fingerprints were all over them."

I tapped my finger to the side of my head. "Angela had it all figured out. She planned for all contingencies. Except for two biggies. Me being annoyingly nosy or Ronnie Schwartzman shooting her dead. Ronnie was a smart guy, but man, was he arrogant. For a long time, he was the golden boy with the Midas touch. Everything went his way. Until his life blew apart when Bunny Frank lit the fuse."

Nana whispered, "Man plans, and God laughs."

I closed my eyes and shivered. "The guy owned the world and now he's lost it all."

Your words and deeds matter. There are consequences to what you say and do. They either exalt you or haunt you, but they will define you and follow you for the rest of your days and beyond. Better get with the program and fast if you want to survive intact. There are no freebies. It's a pay me now or pay me later world, and everything has a price. And one way or another, eventually, we all pay. The price Louis Chennault, Bunny Frank, Ronnie Schwartzman, and Angela Wellborn all paid was a steep one. They paid for their sins with their lives.

The choices we make can come back to haunt us forever, and arrogance will kill you every time. The chaos Bunny Frank's decisions unleashed destroyed many lives. Careers were ruined, three people were dead, and another one will spend the rest of his life behind bars. Such a waste.

Bunny Frank was a force of nature, in many ways she was bigger than life. But in the end, she was no different from the rest of us. She put her panties on one leg at a time. Despite her ruthless quest for control and power, at the end of the day, all she wanted was to be respected and loved. Too bad she never learned respect can't be bought, it has to be earned. Neither Angela nor Bunny understood to be loved, you must be willing to lose your heart but not sell your soul.

I mused, "So if Angela's alibi hadn't been buying perennials, she would have gotten away with it?"

Snip waved a dismissal with a flourish of her elegant hand. "Nah. For a master gardener, she screwed up big time. She should have remembered the importance of the most elementary tool of successful gardening and worn gloves." Sophie Cutler, MD waggled her long, tapered fingers in the air. "No fingerprints. No DNA. No match. No case."

A word about the author…

Born in the Big Apple, Susie Black calls sunny southern California home. Like the protagonist in Death by Sample Size, Susie is a successful apparel sales executive. Susie began telling stories as soon as she learned to talk. Now she's telling all the stories from her garment industry experiences in humorous mysteries.

She reads, writes, and speaks Spanish, albeit with an accent that sounds like Mildred from Michigan went on a Mexican vacation and is trying to fit in with the locals. Since life without pizza and ice cream as her core food groups wouldn't be worth living, she's a dedicated walker to keep her girlish figure. A voracious reader, she's also an avid stamp collector. Susie lives with a highly intelligent man and has one incredibly brainy but smart-aleck adult son who inexplicably blames his sarcasm on an inherited genetic defect.

Looking for more? Reach her at:

mysteries_@authorsusieblack.com

Thank you for purchasing
this publication of The Wild Rose Press, Inc.

For questions or more information
contact us at
info@thewildrosepress.com.

The Wild Rose Press, Inc.
www.thewildrosepress.com

Printed in the USA
CPSIA information can be obtained
at www.ICGtesting.com
LVHW011943260124
769864LV00002B/359